Acting Edition

I0591876

Sherlock Holmes and The American Problem

by R. Hamilton Wright

FOR PRODUCTION INQUIRIES

UNITED STATES AND CANADA
info@concordtheatricals.com
1-866-979-0447

UNITED KINGDOM AND EUROPE
licensing@concordtheatricals.co.uk
020-7054-7298

Each title is subject to availability from Concord Theatricals Corp.,
depending upon country of performance. Please be aware that
SHERLOCK HOLMES AND THE AMERICAN PROBLEM may not be
licensed by Concord Theatricals Corp. in your territory. Professional
and amateur producers should contact the nearest Concord Theatricals
Corp. office or licensing partner to verify availability.

This work is published by Samuel French, an imprint of Concord
Theatricals Corp.

No one shall make any changes in this title(s) for the purpose of production. No part of this book may be reproduced, stored in a retrieval system, scanned, uploaded, or transmitted in any form, by any means, now known or yet to be invented, including mechanical, electronic, digital, photocopying, recording, videotaping, or otherwise, without the prior written permission of the publisher. No one shall share this title(s), or any part of this title(s), through any social media or file hosting websites.

For all inquiries regarding motion picture, television, online/digital and other media rights, please contact Concord Theatricals Corp.

MUSIC AND THIRD-PARTY MATERIALS USE NOTE

Licensees are solely responsible for obtaining formal written permission from copyright owners to use copyrighted music and/or other copyrighted third-party materials (e.g., artworks, logos) in the performance of this play and are strongly cautioned to do so. If no such permission is obtained by the licensee, then the licensee must use only original music and materials that the licensee owns and controls. Licensees are solely responsible and liable for clearances of all third-party copyrighted materials, including without limitation music, and shall indemnify the copyright owners of the play(s) and their licensing agent, Concord Theatricals Corp., against any costs, expenses, losses and liabilities arising from the use of such copyrighted third-party materials by licensees. For music, please contact the appropriate music licensing authority in your territory for the rights to any incidental music.

IMPORTANT BILLING AND CREDIT REQUIREMENTS

If you have obtained performance rights to this title, please refer to your licensing agreement for important billing and credit requirements.

SHERLOCK HOLMES AND THE AMERICAN PROBLEM was first produced by Seattle Rep (Braden Abraham, Artistic Director; Jeffrey Herrmann, Managing Director) in Seattle, Washington on April 22, 2016. The performance was directed by Allison Narver, with sets, lights, and projections by L.B. Morse, costumes by Deb Trout, original music and sound by Obadiah Eaves, fight direction by Rick Sordelet, dialect coaching by Gin Hammond, production dramaturgy by Kristin Leahey, and assistant scenic design by Nick Passafiume. The production stage manager was Michael B. Paul. The cast was as follows:

MR. SHERLOCK HOLMES . . . . Darragh Kennan

DR. JOHN WATSON . . . . .Andrew McGinn

MRS. HUDSON . . . . Marianne Owen

MISS PHOEBE ANNE MOSES . . . . Christine Marie Brown

MISS CHARLOTTE LICHTER /

"MAYHEM" MAGGIE MALLOY .Cheyenne Casebier

MR. MYCROFT HOLMES . . . . Charles Leggett

THE PINKERTON . . . . Alex Matthews

MAJOR THADDEUS ISAAC RAMSEY . . . . Rob Burgess

ARNOLD CROFTERS / RED HOOK BOYLE / ENSEMBLE . . Tim Gouran

CHARACTERS

(with possible doubling)

MR. SHERLOCK HOLMES – A Consulting Detective

DR. JOHN WATSON – his Friend and Colleague

MRS. HUDSON – their Housekeeper

MISS PHOEBE ANNE MOSES – a Young American Woman

MISS CHARLOTTE LICHTER – an American Mining Engineer /
"MAYHEM" MAGGIE MALLOY – an American Criminal

MR. MYCROFT HOLMES – Sherlock's Older Brother /
JEFFERSON HENRY – an American Criminal

THE PINKERTON – an American Detective

MAJOR THADDEUS ISAAC RAMSEY – an Army Tutor /
DUBBY CONROY – an American Thug

RED HOOK BOYLE – an American Thug /
CAPTAIN FLEMING – an Army Officer /
THE AMERICAN AMBASSADOR

SETTING

London

TIME

June, 1887

AUTHOR'S NOTES

In the premiere at the Seattle Repertory Theatre this play was performed
by nine actors: six men and three women.

ACT I

(In the dark we hear and feel a deep rumbling pass beneath our feet. Then.)

Prologue

*(Night. A lonely street in London. A **MAN** runs on and it is obvious that he is running away from something or someone. He is panicked, out of breath; he stumbles and falls. We notice his conservative, well-cut clothing is torn in a few places.)*

CROFTERS. This can't be happening to me. How in God's name can this be happening to someone like me? I should never have turned away from Mr. Holmes.

(He hears something, gets up and looks back desperately whence he came.)

Who are you? You...you must have the wrong man. My name is Crofters, Arnold Crofters. I just work at the Bank. What do you want? The printing plates? I don't have them! I swear. The American has them!

(He takes a few hesitant steps.)

Someone help me. Please! Someone help me!

(They are coming for him.)

No, no, please...you don't need to do this, you mustn't... no!

(A hideous scream is heard.)

(Lights fade to:)

Scene One

(The next day. Hyde Park. A lovely morning in June. Seated on a bench, dressed in a summer suit of some sort but with what looks like a lap blanket around his shoulders, is **MR. SHERLOCK HOLMES***. He is trying his best to listen to the birds in the trees above his head. But other things are in his head. Then – a* **YOUNG WOMAN** *enters. She is dressed beautifully and seems on edge.)*

MOSES. Mr. Holmes? Mr. Sherlock Holmes?

*(***HOLMES*** opens his eyes.)*

HOLMES. Miss Moses?

MOSES. Yes. Miss Phoebe Ann Moses, Mr. Holmes.

(He stands. She offers her hand. He takes it.)

Thank you so much for taking the time to meet me and at such an early hour.

HOLMES. Yes. Well. Shall we sit?

MOSES. I'm afraid I don't have much time, Mr. Holmes.

HOLMES. Still, I think we should sit.

MOSES. All right.

(They sit. He watches her for a moment. The birds sing.)

HOLMES. You indicated, in your rather brief letter to me, that you might be in need of my services.

MOSES. Yes. Mr. Holmes, I want you to find my brother.

HOLMES. Oh. Your brother.

MOSES. Yes.

HOLMES. Hmm. And he is?

MOSES. Solomon is his name. Solomon Moses. He is my older brother. He came to London from New York a little over three years ago. And shortly after he got here he just – dropped out of sight. We haven't heard from him since. We've been very worried about him, Mr. Holmes.

HOLMES. When you say "we," you are speaking of your family back in Ohio?

MOSES. Yes, that's right – *(Suddenly wary.)* How in the world did you know that?

HOLMES. Like many Americans, Miss Moses, you apparently do not believe you have an accent.

MOSES. Oh, I see. Well, you are right on the money, Mr. Holmes. Ohio born and bred.

HOLMES. Tell me, why did your brother – Solomon – emigrate?

MOSES. He was – He... I'm not going to lie to you, Mr. Holmes.

HOLMES. Is that a promise?

MOSES. Yes, of course.

HOLMES. Thank you, Miss Moses. Phoebe Ann Moses. *(He gazes at her for a moment.)* Did you know your name is golden and hums like a hive of bees?

MOSES. I'm sorry?

HOLMES. What would you say, Miss Moses, if I told you that I sometimes hear colour and taste sound? *(A breath.)*

MOSES. I would say you are either very clever or quite mad.

HOLMES. *(A smile.)* Ah. Yes. Now, your brother...?

MOSES.   Well. Solomon was in the war. He was a demolitions engineer in Grant's Army. When he came home – he was...well, he was not the same man, Mr. Holmes. He went off to New York and eventually got himself into a great deal of trouble there. I'm afraid that he had been arrested more than a few times.

HOLMES. He left America because of the threat of prison?

MOSES. Yes. Well... I think so. I'm ashamed to admit that we hadn't communicated for a very long while.

HOLMES. Not communicating with an elder brother. At worst a venial sin, Miss Moses.

MOSES. Mr. Holmes –

HOLMES. What was your brother's last known address in London?

> *(She takes an envelope out of her reticule and hands it to* **HOLMES.***)*

MOSES. I'm very sorry, Mr. Holmes, but as I said I really don't have much time. All the information I have about Solomon is in this envelope.

HOLMES. Miss Moses –

MOSES. Along with a check for one hundred pounds.

HOLMES. My fees are set, Miss Moses.

MOSES. Oh, I am sorry. Is that not enough?

HOLMES. Of course it is. It is much more than enough. That in itself is intriguing but beside the point. You see, I have not yet decided to take on your case.

MOSES. Oh, but you must, Mr. Holmes. Please. I'm depending on you. *(She touches his arm.)* I believe my brother may be in terrible danger.

HOLMES. From whom?

MOSES. I don't know. His... His associates, maybe.

HOLMES. With whom does he associate?

MOSES. All the information I have is in –

> *(He rises as if to leave and she stands.)*

HOLMES. Miss Moses, I am afraid I can't –

MOSES. Do you have brothers and sisters, Mr. Holmes?

HOLMES. No. Well, yes. I have – an older brother.

MOSES. Then you understand.

HOLMES. You should not assume that I do.

MOSES. Please find Solomon for me.

HOLMES. Where are you staying in London?

MOSES. No, I'm sorry, Mr. Holmes, but I'm afraid that I will have to contact you.

HOLMES. You promised not to lie to me!

MOSES. But I haven't lied.

HOLMES. No? You allow me to believe you live in Ohio but your dress, hat and shoes – all of the finest quality but none of them new – were fashioned in New York. You call yourself "Miss" but have neglected to remove your wedding band. You obviously feel that you are being followed. Who would be following you, *Miss* Moses? And why?

MOSES. You are very clever and I am sorry if I have deceived you but please, Mr. Holmes, I beg you – find my brother. Find Solomon Moses.

> *(She rushes out.)*

HOLMES. Solomon Moses.

> *(A man enters, walking in the same direction as* **MISS MOSES.** *This is the* **PINKERTON.** *He bumps into* **HOLMES.***)*

PINKS. Sorry, mack.

*(The **PINKERTON** – having taken a piece of paper from Holmes' pocket – exits in the direction taken by **MISS MOSES** and **HOLMES** looks after him.)*

(Music. And with the music there is now a sort of promenade in which we see most of the characters we will meet in this story. **HOLMES** might observe all of them even though this may not be happening in "real" time. He may be buffeted and jostled by these people as they make their way through the streets of London. This is simply a suggestion of what might occur:)*

*(A young woman enters as **HOLMES** watches the **PINKERTON** depart – this is **CHARLOTTE LICHTER**, and she comes from the same direction that **MISS MOSES** exited. She has a visitor's map of London in her hand and is obviously trying to find her way to an address in a strange city. **PHOEBE ANN MOSES** crosses upstage, aware that someone is following her. The **PINKERTON** shadows her. From another direction a **MAN** enters. He is dressed impeccably in a dark suit. This is **MYCROFT HOLMES** and as he observes **MISS LICHTER** from a distance he drops the newspaper he was carrying. **MISS LICHTER** bumps into **SHERLOCK HOLMES** and as she begins to walk away **ANOTHER MAN** appears, also in a dark suit but with*

---

* A license to produce *Sherlock Holmes and The American Problem* does not include a performance license for any third-party or copyrighted music. Licensees should create an original composition or use music in the public domain. For further information, please see the Music and Third Party Materials Use Note on page iii.

his left sleeve pinned up as he has lost that arm. He smokes a briar pipe. This is the **AMERICAN AMBASSADOR.** **MYCROFT** *looks in the direction of where* **CHARLOTTE LICHTER** *is departing and* **ANOTHER MAN** *appears who has a bag of birdseed and is feeding pigeons as he walks along a path. This is one* **MAJOR THADDEUS ISAAC RAMSEY.** *He picks up the newspaper dropped by* **MYCROFT HOLMES** *and returns it to him.* **MYCROFT** *then follows the* **AMERICAN AMBASSADOR** *as that man departs.* **HOLMES** *– his head full of too many images, walks off towards:)*

Scene Two

(The sitting room of the apartments at 221B Baker Street, the lodgings of Mr. Sherlock Holmes and Dr. John Watson. **WATSON** *is having his breakfast and reading the morning paper.* **MRS. HUDSON** *attends.)*

MRS. HUDSON. Some more coffee, Doctor?

WATSON. Oh, yes. Thank you.

MRS. HUDSON. How are the scones this morning?

WATSON. As always, Mrs. Hudson, they are sublime.

MRS. HUDSON. I'm glad.

WATSON. And I really must stop eating them.

MRS. HUDSON. Oh?

WATSON. Someday.

MRS. HUDSON. Yes.

WATSON. Holmes? Is he still in bed?

MRS. HUDSON. No, Doctor. No. I think he's actually out and about this morning.

WATSON. Really?

MRS. HUDSON. Yes. When I brought up the breakfast things he had already gone.

WATSON. Oh, good. Good. I hope it is good.

MRS. HUDSON. Yes.

WATSON. He has been out all night, every night for the past... I don't know how long.

MRS. HUDSON. It's been a fortnight, Doctor.

WATSON. Really?

HUDSON. Since we have had him at breakfast.

WATSON. Yes, and then he sleeps all day and I...well I have been a bit concerned.

HUDSON. Yes, I know. *(A breath.)* Doctor, did you see they've closed the Bank?

WATSON. The Bank of England?

MRS. HUDSON. Yes. Because of that gas explosion in Cheapside a fortnight ago. Apparently, they're concerned about the very foundation of the building.

WATSON. Oh dear.

> *(HOLMES comes into the room like a hurricane, stripping off his blanket and hat and throwing them every which way. MRS. HUDSON scurries about trying to keep up with him.)*

HOLMES. What a ridiculous morning!

WATSON. Ah, there you are –

HOLMES. Coffee!

WATSON. Good morning, Holmes.

HOLMES. What is the point in going out at all, I ask you?

MRS. HUDSON. I'll just get a fresh pot.

> *(She exits.)*

WATSON. Holmes, did you see they've closed the Bank of England?

HOLMES. It is impossible!

WATSON. No, it says quite clearly here in the *Times* –

HOLMES. I would be the first to admit, Watson, that the Queen's fiftieth year on her throne is worthy of a celebration.

WATSON. Oh, I see.

HOLMES. I would even go so far as to allow that a national holiday might be in order. But...this?

WATSON. What is it now, Holmes?

HOLMES. We have been invaded, Watson. From the far corners of the Empire and beyond, tens of thousands of well-wishers flood the city – all here to congratulate our Gracious Queen on her Golden Jubilee. Meanwhile, it has become impossible to move about the city! Every thoroughfare is chock-a-block with tourists and Princes and Rajahs and Nabobs.

WATSON. Oh come now, Holmes, it's only for a fortnight or so. Surely a little inconvenience –

HOLMES. It is not just inconvenient, Watson. This swelling of the metropolis has had serious consequences.

WATSON. Oh really. How so?

HOLMES. Only yesterday I was pursuing a very promising lead in my present investigation – in the person of one Arnold Crofters, a senior clerk at the Bank of England – when he eluded me by simply crossing Regent Street.

WATSON. Holmes, the Bank of –

HOLMES. At that very instant a contingent of Canadian Mounted Police came clopping by and as I was unable to negotiate their number, I lost my man.

WATSON. Was this man –

HOLMES. But the worst of the lot, Watson, are the Americans!

WATSON. What's wrong with the Americans?

HOLMES. What is right with them? They throng the streets, staring off into space like ruminating cattle, they block your path, they jostle you and no matter how fetching their aspect, how charming their smile – they lie to your face!

WATSON. Really?

HOLMES. And they're everywhere! Here, here, for instance –

(He picks up the newspaper.)

"Mr. Mark Twain, the celebrated author of *The Innocents Abroad* and creator of Tom Sawyer and Huckleberry Finn" – whoever they are – "offers a program of humorous recollections of his life on the Mississippi River at Guildhall tonight at eight o'clock." Sounds fascinating.

WATSON. He is quite amusing, you know. I read *A Connecticut Yankee* –

HOLMES. And most egregious of all – featured ad nauseum in every newspaper and plastered on every spare wall – Buffalo Bill's Wild West! 100 Riders! 200 Animals! Including the thundering, stampeding Buffalo!

WATSON. Bison, actually.

HOLMES. Red Indians! Cowboys! The Deadwood Stage. Little Sure Shot, the Queen of the Sharpshooters, Miss Annie Oakley!

(He turns the page.)

WATSON. Deadwood Stage. Hah.

HOLMES. Here. "Buffalo Bill Boosted by Bedford" – what tripe – "Colonel William F. Cody, famously known as Buffalo Bill, will exchange his fringed buckskins for evening attire at a gala dinner to be held in his honor at Bedford House. Miss Annie Oakley and the American Ambassador will be among the guests." *(Turns page.)*

WATSON. Fringed buckskins!

HOLMES. "Visiting Buffalo Frightened by Rare Earthquake: A series of small earthquakes centered in Victoria Street rumbled through Westminster yesterday morning, rattling cups and saucers from Whitehall to Chelsea. In Earls Court, the herd of American Buffalo became agitated and briefly stampeded, flattening a tent. No injuries were reported." A pity that.

WATSON. Not actually buffalo, you know – American bison.

HOLMES. Earthquakes!

(He tosses the paper down.)

We never have earthquakes. Probably the Buffalo's fault as well –

HOLMES & WATSON. Bison!

HOLMES. – all this stampeding about.

WATSON. As you say, Holmes; too many Americans.

*(**HOLMES** drinks his coffee.)*

HOLMES. And the coffee's gone cold. Mrs. Hudson!

*(**MRS. HUDSON** enters with a pot of coffee.)*

MRS. HUDSON. Mr. Holmes –

HOLMES. Mrs. Hudson, were you lurking outside our door?

MRS. HUDSON. I do not lurk, Mr. Holmes. A telegram for you.

HOLMES. Oh. Hmmm.

(He takes the telegram.)

And some fresh coffee, if you please.

MRS. HUDSON. Yes, sir.

(As she puts down the new pot, she shares a glance with **WATSON**.*)*

HOLMES. *(Reading telegram.)* Damn.

WATSON. What is it?

HOLMES. Inspector Lestrade. Mrs. Hudson, I will not be in for dinner this evening.

MRS. HUDSON. Very well, Mr. Holmes.

(She turns to exit.)

WATSON. Oh, as a matter of fact, Mrs. Hudson, neither will I. Thank you.

MRS. HUDSON. Thank *you*, gentlemen. I shall spend the evening at my sister's, then. We're hoping to see The Wild West in the next few days.

(She exits.)

WATSON. What does Lestrade have to say?

HOLMES. The man I was following – Crofters.

WATSON. The bank clerk?

HOLMES. Yes. He is dead.

WATSON. How did he die?

HOLMES. He was stabbed. Last night.

WATSON. Good Lord. A banker?

HOLMES. Not just a banker, Watson. I have suspected for some time that Crofters was the conduit between the criminal underworld and the City's financial institutions.

WATSON. Heavens.

HOLMES. And his is the second killing.

WATSON. The second? Who was the first?

HOLMES. His name was Lee Wu Chang. The undisputed master of the opium trade, known throughout London as "The Emperor of Limehouse."

WATSON. Was he stabbed as well?

HOLMES. Yes. In precisely the same fashion.

WATSON. When was this?

HOLMES. A fortnight ago.

WATSON. Does Scotland Yard think these murders are connected?

HOLMES. What the police think as they chase their own tails I cannot imagine.

WATSON. Do *you* think they are connected?

HOLMES. In all probability nothing more than an interesting coincidence.

WATSON. You've told me you don't believe in coincidences.

HOLMES. When they are invoked to justify shoddy thinking, I do not.

WATSON. Holmes, I didn't know you were working on a case.

HOLMES. I'm not, really.

WATSON. But you just said –

HOLMES. I mean it is not an actual case, Watson – I have no client.

WATSON. Then what is it?

HOLMES. I'm not sure. Something is hiding, Watson. Something intricate is hiding beneath the cacophony and hurly-burly of the Jubilee. At times I can almost see it. Almost taste it. It is a kind of...checkered thing.

WATSON. Checkered?

HOLMES. And I have begun to sense a presence.

WATSON. What do you mean?

HOLMES. There is a very real character behind these occurrences.

WATSON. You mean an individual's character?

HOLMES. I tell you, Watson, I can feel him. It's infuriating. It is almost as if he has been toying with me.

WATSON. Who?

HOLMES. I have no idea. But I sense that he is playing a very deep game. *(A breath.)* If I didn't know better, I'd think it was Mycroft.

WATSON. Your brother?

> *(A woman dressed well but for business rushes in. She is* **CHARLOTTE LICHTER** *and looks to be at her wit's end.* **MRS. HUDSON** *trails behind her.)*

LICHTER. Mr. Holmes!

MRS. HUDSON. Please, miss, you mustn't! –

LICHTER. Mr. Sherlock Holmes –

MRS. HUDSON. – you can't just –

LICHTER. – you've got to help me! Please. Please, Mr. Holmes. They've taken it. They've stolen the Mole!

> *(She stumbles and collapses to the floor.)*

WATSON. Hello! Careful there –

MRS. HUDSON. Oh dear!

> *(***WATSON** *goes to her and feels her pulse, etc.)*

I'm so sorry, gentlemen.

HOLMES. That's quite all right, Mrs. Hudson. Another one of these headstrong American women, apparently. How is she, Watson?

WATSON. Her breathing is shallow and her pulse is a bit rapid. Simple exhaustion, I should say. Let's get her to a chair.

> (**WATSON** *and* **HOLMES** *carry the woman to a chair.*)

HOLMES. Mrs. Hudson, a brandy if you please.

> (*She pours a brandy. The woman comes to as they sit her down.*)

LICHTER. What is...? Oh, I'm... I'm so sorry... I've...

WATSON. That's quite all right. Please – sit quietly.

> (**MRS. HUDSON** *brings the brandy.*)

LICHTER. Oh, Lord, I feel like such a fool.

WATSON. No, no, you mustn't.

LICHTER. I'm not the fainting type, gentlemen, I assure you.

WATSON. Of course you're not.

HOLMES. And yet you did faint.

LICHTER. Is that one of your legendary skills, Mr. Holmes – stating the obvious?

WATSON. Oh dear.

HOLMES. Drink that.

LICHTER. No, please. I am sorry, but I... I haven't slept or eaten since I found out, that's why I fainted – Mr. Holmes! They've taken the Mole!

WATSON. Here, have some brandy.

LICHTER. No, I'm fine, really. Mr. Holmes –

HOLMES. This man is a doctor.

LICHTER. Thank you, doctor, but I need –

WATSON. What you need, madam, is food and rest.

LICHTER. I know, I know all that but I've got to tell you –

HOLMES. Mrs. Hudson bring some toast, will you?

MRS. HUDSON. Of course.

LICHTER. Please –

MRS. HUDSON. With butter?

HOLMES. I should think so. Watson?

WATSON. Yes, fine.

HOLMES. With butter!

LICHTER. Mr. Holmes, please, you've got to listen –

WATSON. And some marmalade as well, Mrs. Hudson.

MRS. HUDSON. Very good, doctor.

LICHTER. Dammnit, gentlemen, will you please listen to me?

> (**HOLMES** *and* **WATSON** *are stunned into silence for just a moment.*)

MRS. HUDSON. Of course they will, my dear. But first, as the doctor has ordered, you must eat something. The marmalade is my own, you know.

LICHTER. Oh. Well... Thank you, ma'am. Thank you.

> (*She eats a bite of toast and butter and jam.*)

WATSON. Yes, thank you, Mrs. Hudson.

> (**MRS. HUDSON** *exits.*)

HOLMES. Now, are you able to tell us your name?

LICHTER. Of course, I am – Lichter. Charlotte Lichter.

HOLMES. Charlotte Lichter. Now, Mrs. – sorry – Miss Lichter, I can see that you've spent your morning near the St. Katherine Docks and that you are an American of German heritage who graduated from the University of California where you trained as an...as an engineer? and now make your home in San Francisco where you currently indulge your fondness for both Persian cats and Asiatic lilies.

LICHTER. How on earth –

HOLMES. Your boots.

LICHTER. My boots?

HOLMES. Then the sand on your boots; the badge on your purse; the callous on your right index finger and the slide rule in your reticule which promotes the callous; your lapel pin; the ring on your right hand, the lack of one on your left; your bracelet; the cat hair on your coat and the slight residue of pollen on your cuffs.

LICHTER. That's amazing –

HOLMES. I only state the obvious.

LICHTER. Mr. Holmes, please –

WATSON. Are you really an engineer, Miss Lichter?

LICHTER. Yes, Doctor, I really am.

WATSON. Extraordinary. Well done.

LICHTER. Thank you.

HOLMES. Now, Miss Lichter, tell me what I do not know – what has happened and how may I help you?

LICHTER. Mr. Holmes, somebody stole my Mole.

HOLMES. Your mole?

LICHTER. Yes. All five tons of it.

HOLMES. Ha!

WATSON. A five ton mole?

LICHTER. That's right. Crated up in New York and shipped to the St. Katherine Docks where it arrived two weeks ago, on the thirty-first. I arrived yesterday. The Mole was to be put on the train to Earl's Court yesterday morning where it was to be reassembled and displayed as part of the American Exhibition, but when the dock manager came to get it, it was gone.

HOLMES. When did it go missing?

LICHTER. We don't know. Sometime in the last two weeks.

HOLMES. Miss Lichter, what precisely has been lost?

LICHTER. Oh, yes, of course. Well. The Mole is a self-propelled, steam-powered tunneling device of my own design which, while protecting the excavators inside a steel hull, reinforces the tunnel itself as the Mole progresses.

WATSON. You designed this marvelous machine all by yourself?

LICHTER. Yes, Doctor. All by myself.

WATSON. Remarkable.

HOLMES. Is it worth a great deal?

LICHTER. Yes, I have patents on several original features of the Mole.

HOLMES. You think that some industrial competitor might have stolen your machine to gain access to its innovations?

LICHTER. I can't think of any other reason.

HOLMES. No?

WATSON. Perhaps someone wanted to tunnel somewhere.

(**HOLMES** *and* **LICHTER** *look at* **WATSON.**)

HOLMES. Yes, Miss Lichter. I will look into this for you. It is an intriguing little problem.

LICHTER. Thank you, Mr. Holmes, thank you very much.

HOLMES. Where are you staying in London?

LICHTER. I'm at Morley's Hotel. But I want to help, Mr. Holmes. I can –

(She stands and teeters, **WATSON** *catches her.)*

WATSON. Steady, now. Miss Lichter, I insist that you return to your hotel, have a late breakfast and go immediately to bed.

LICHTER. But I –

HOLMES. You really must do as the doctor says. I will contact you at your hotel tomorrow morning. I should have something for you by then.

(MRS. HUDSON returns.)

MRS. HUDSON. Mr. Holmes.

HOLMES. Yes, Mrs. Hudson?

MRS. HUDSON. *(Quite amazed.)* Your brother is here.

(A soberly, but beautifully dressed man is right behind her. A moment of stillness.)

HOLMES. Mycroft?

MYCROFT. Pardon the intrusion, Sherlock. I didn't know you had a visitor.

LICHTER. I'm just on my way out, sir. Thank you again, Mr. Holmes.

WATSON. See that you eat something.

LICHTER. I will, Doctor. *(To* **HOLMES***.)* Please find it for me, Mr. Holmes. My whole life is wrapped up in it. *(To* **MRS. HUDSON***.)* And thank you for the toast ma'am. The jam was delicious.

MRS. HUDSON. Thank you, my dear. And see that you do get some rest.

(MISS LICHTER *exits with* MRS. HUDSON.)

MYCROFT. A little early in the day for female American... engineers?

HOLMES. Business.

MYCROFT. Oh? Something about lilies?

HOLMES. She's lost something.

MYCROFT. Her cat?

HOLMES. No, something else.

MYCROFT. And will you find it for her?

HOLMES. We shall see.

(*A breath.*)

MYCROFT. You look surprised to see me, Sherlock.

HOLMES. Of course I am.

MYCROFT. Is it so unusual that a man should visit his younger brother?

HOLMES. You know it is, Mycroft. You've never been to my rooms. Ever.

MYCROFT. That is not purely true, you know. I distinctly recall having a conversation with you in your rooms.

HOLMES. No. Never.

MYCROFT. Yes. I remember it quite clearly. We discussed at some length our concerns over Nanny's possible relationship with Barker.

HOLMES. Barker? The gardener?

MYCROFT. I believe he was the head groundskeeper.

HOLMES. Mycroft, I was six.

MYCROFT. Yes, and I was twelve and I came to *your* room. So, you see?

HOLMES. How may I help you, brother?

MYCROFT. I was just on my way to the office, and thought I would deliver this in person.

> *(He hands* **HOLMES** *an engraved invitation.* **HOLMES** *opens it.)*

MYCROFT. Good morning, Dr. Watson.

WATSON. And a good morning to you, Mr. Holmes. Would you care for some coffee?

MYCROFT. Thank you, Doctor, perhaps another time. I'm afraid I'm in something of a rush this morning.

HOLMES. "Mr. Alfred de Rothschild requests the pleasure of your company at a private exhibition of oil paintings on canvas by Emile Vernet." Uncle Emile?

MYCROFT. Great-Uncle Emile.

HOLMES. "One Seamore Place. Mayfair. Nine o'clock. Thursday night."

WATSON. Who is Emile Vernet?

HOLMES. My grandmother's brother.

MYCROFT. Our mother's favorite uncle.

HOLMES. French painter of some repute.

MYCROFT. Large, military subjects, for the most part.

HOLMES. Battles and such. Very colorful.

MYCROFT. Very large.

> *(A breath.)*

HOLMES. Mycroft.

MYCROFT. Yes?

HOLMES. Prepare yourself.

MYCROFT. Oh, Sherlock. Please. No.

HOLMES. Yes. *Yes*. Emile Vernet.

> *(The two men look at each other almost as if in a duel.* **WATSON** *– although completely perplexed – knows well enough to leave them alone. Finally:)*

MYCROFT. Mervin Leeet.

HOLMES. Merit Levene.

MYCROFT. Nevil Meeter.

HOLMES. Everet Milne.

MYCROFT. You win. Now, Sherlock, please be serious –

HOLMES. By all means, brother, let us be serious. You are planning to attend this "exhibition"?

MYCROFT. Yes. Yes, I am. We're family, after all. I was hoping I could convince you to come as well. And Dr. Watson, of course.

WATSON. Oh, yes. Well. Bound to be good wine.

MYCROFT. Hmm?

WATSON. The Rothchilds. Good wine, I imagine.

MYCROFT. Oh, absolutely. What do you say, Sherlock?

HOLMES. Thursday? Tomorrow night?

MYCROFT. Yes. I realize it's short notice, of course. But still – Uncle Emile.

HOLMES. Great-Uncle Emile.

MYCROFT. And I think having both of us there would have meant a great deal to mother.

HOLMES. Mother?

MYCROFT. Yes. She was Emile's favorite niece, you know.

HOLMES. Yes.

MYCROFT. And after father died –

HOLMES. I know, Mycroft.

MYCROFT. *(Placing his hand on* **HOLMES'** *shoulder.)* Then may I count on you, brother?

HOLMES. Yes. Yes, of course we'll come. We'll see you there.

MYCROFT. Capital. Well, I must be off. See you tomorrow, then. Dr. Watson.

WATSON. Good day, Mr. Holmes.

> *(***MYCROFT** *pauses at the door. He looks intently at* **HOLMES.***)*

MYCROFT. Sherlock?

HOLMES. Yes?

MYCROFT. What do you make of this?

> *(He tosses a briar pipe to* **HOLMES,** *who catches it and then spends a moment looking it over, first with his naked eye and then with a small magnifying glass he takes from his pocket.)*

HOLMES. Other than the obvious, there's not much here.

MYCROFT. No?

HOLMES. Well, the pipe is English briar but its owner is American.

> *(He scrapes a bit of charred ash from the bowl with a penknife. He smells and tastes the ash.)*

Yes. The tobacco is a Cavendish with a bit of Burley. So. He is right handed. Lives... Eastern Seaboard. North of Virginia. Has a dog. A terrier. He drinks. Sometimes to excess.

MYCROFT. The dog?

HOLMES. Ha! Portly. In his fifties? Fought for the Union, of course. And...this may be extending myself a little, but...missing his left arm? Or at least the use of it?

(**HOLMES** *hands the pipe back to his brother.*)

MYCROFT. As you say, not much there. But here, you see?

(*He shows* **HOLMES** *something on the pipe's stem.*)

HOLMES. Ah. Yes, of course. He fishes.

MYCROFT. For?

HOLMES. Trout.

MYCROFT. Yes?

HOLMES. Possibly salmon.

MYCROFT. Good.

HOLMES. How long was he in Scotland?

MYCROFT. Who?

HOLMES. The American Ambassador.

MYCROFT. Very good.

HOLMES. He is missing his left arm, isn't he?

MYCROFT. Yes, I am sure he misses it a great deal.

HOLMES. Mycroft –

MYCROFT. The Ambassador spent a week in the Highlands and returned to London yesterday afternoon.

HOLMES. Of course. He wouldn't want to miss the gala reception at Bedford House for *Buffalo Bill*.

MYCROFT. Quite.

> (**SHERLOCK** *turns away from his brother.*)

I shall see you both tomorrow evening. Nine o'clock. Remember, Sherlock: For Mother – don't be late.

> (**MYCROFT** *exits.*)

HOLMES. I hate it when he puts me through my paces like that!

> (**WATSON** *is looking at the invitation.*)

WATSON. It was good of him to deliver the invitation in person.

HOLMES. Alfred de Rothschild. My brother would detest this sort of thing even more than I.

WATSON. Holmes, you once told me that your brother spends most of his time at The Diogenes Club.

HOLMES. Yes.

WATSON. But he just said he was on his way to the "office." What office?

HOLMES. In Whitehall.

WATSON. Oh, he's in the government, then?

HOLMES. Yes. No. Well...the fact is Mycroft oversees a small department in the Home Office that technically does not exist.

WATSON. Really? What do they do?

HOLMES. I am afraid I cannot tell you.

WATSON. Oh. Well, that sounds rather secretive.

HOLMES. Yes, Mycroft's work has always been a bit on the shadowy side.

> (**HOLMES** *is looking at the invitation.* **WATSON** *finishes up his coffee.*)

WATSON. And what was all that about "Nevil Meeter" and "Everet Milne"?

HOLMES. Oh. A game we played as boys. Our mother called it our "anagramantics."

WATSON. Oh, I see. Oh, yes, of course – Emile Vernet... Neville...

HOLMES. Yes. Whenever we met someone for the first time – especially if it was a person of some authority – vicar, head master, prime minister, what have you – we would construct an anagram of their name. Had to be plausible.

WATSON. Brothers.

HOLMES. Yes. I was always better at it than Mycroft so he never wants to play.

WATSON. Well, I must get started, I have patients to see.

HOLMES. Hmmm.

WATSON. Holmes, do you need my assistance tonight?

HOLMES. Tonight?

WATSON. I can change my plans, you know.

HOLMES. No, no. I thank you for the kind offer, Watson, but I don't expect that I'll need you tonight.

WATSON. Well, in case you change your mind – I'm having dinner at my club.

HOLMES. Capital.

WATSON. And you?

HOLMES. What about me?

WATSON. What are your plans for the evening? You told Mrs. Hudson you would be out.

HOLMES. Oh. Yes. I'm not sure, Watson. Perhaps I shall go to the Guildhall and hear Mr. Mark Twain's humorous discourse of his life on the Mississippi.

WATSON. Right.

> (**WATSON** *exits to his room.* **HOLMES** *is left, thinking.*)

HOLMES. Americans. Phoebe Anne Moses and her brother Solomon. Charlotte Lichter and her mechanical mole. The American Ambassador and his briar pipe. *(A breath.)* There's a swath of green fluttering – shot through with blue that is cold like clay. Americans. The American.

> *(Lights change. We transition into:)*

Scene Three

(That night. Near the river. Sounds of the London docks: Fog horns, bells on barges, etc. A man enters. He is dressed somewhat flamboyantly. This is one **JEFFERSON HENRY**. *He is an American. He is in a hurry. His* **TWO COMPANIONS**, *who are dressed like roughnecks, are gabbing as they walk along.)*

DUBBY. So I said to her, but I like your pants and she hauled off and popped me again!

BOYLE. Dees English broads are nuts, I tell ya.

DUBBY. But I liked her pants and I said so – what's to get all hot about?

JEFF. Hey, you two monkeys keep quiet. Jesus, you're just as bad as you were five years ago. Haven't ya learned anything? You're on the job.

BOYLE & DUBBY. Sorry, Solly.

JEFF. So shut it. Both of you. You know what Mayhem said: You say nothin' about nothin' to no one. You do this one last thing, you're paid off and on the next scow back to the Bowery. You got it?

DUBBY & BOYLE. Yeah, yeah, we got it, Solly.

JEFF. All right. Red Hook – is he still with us?

BOYLE. I think so.

JEFF. You think so?

BOYLE. I mean, he's real good, Solly, whoever he is. Like a ghost. If you hadn't told me to look for a tail I'd a never seen him.

JEFF. Well, this is as good a spot as any. Let's do this. And boys – remember, we gotta draw this gent out so play it to the hilt, right? Like you're really tryin' to kill me.

BOYLE. We know, Solly

DUBBY. Yeah – to the hilt.

JEFF. Allright, on three. One, two, three.

> *(The* **TWO BODYGUARDS** *take out their knives and start circling* **JEFFERSON***, who speaks up.)*

Hey, hey, hey what the hell is this?

> *(They move closer to him, their knives out.)*

If this is some kind of joke, boys, it ain't funny. You put those shanks away!

> *(Closer still.)*

Don't be stupid, boys. If you do this it'll get back to you-know-who and you'll both be good as dead!

> *(They grab him.)*

No! *(Then, sotto voce.)* Careful boys, this suit cost me a hunnerd bucks. No!

> *(Suddenly* **SHERLOCK HOLMES** *appears. He blows a police whistle. The attackers turn.)*

HOLMES. Gentlemen. Release that man. The police are on their way.

> *(As if on cue we hear police whistles not far away. The* **TWO THUGS** *lower their knives.)*

JEFF. You're Sherlock Holmes?

HOLMES. Yes and you are Jefferson Henry.

DUBBY. *(Laughing.)* Jefferson Henry? That's what ya call yerself in London, Solly?

BOYLE. Hey, what's wrong with Solomon Moses?

HOLMES. Solomon Moses?

JEFF. Shut up you two!

HOLMES. You are Solomon Moses?

JEFF. That's right, mister. The last man you'll ever talk to. Okay, boys, do your job!

BOYLE. Whatever you say, Solly.

DUBBY. To the hilt!

(The two men then stab SOLOMON MOSES several times each.)

JEFF. No, no, no! I had immunity!

(They release the corpse and turn to HOLMES, who backs away in a defensive crouch, but his attackers move quickly to cut off his retreat. He is caught. They attack, apparently unconcerned with the police whistles getting nearer. HOLMES parries their initial attacks, but his adversaries are relentless, pressing their advantage. HOLMES is cut across the forearm. They sense his weakening and begin to advance for the kill when out of the dark another man appears, entering the fray like a bull. It is the PINKERTON. The fight continues for a time – now two against two, but the tide has turned: a knife skitters across the pavement as an arm is shattered, a jaw broken. The two assassins limp off quickly leaving HOLMES and his ally back to back, breathing hard, their fists still raised.)

(A moment.)

HOLMES. If I may ask – have we met before?

(His new ally regards him for a moment.)

PINKS. Beat it.

HOLMES. I beg your pardon?

> *(A shot rings out, a bullet hits the man in the upper arm. He grunts.)*

PINKS. Ah, goddammit! Go!

> *(He pushes **HOLMES** aside as another shot is heard. A bullet ricochets off the pavement. He pulls a revolver from his coat and walks in the direction of the gunshots, firing the pistol as he advances. **HOLMES** stumbles off in the other direction.)*

> *(Lights shift to:)*

Scene Four

(Baker Street. The flat is in shadow. Gaslight through the windows. A door opens and closes. There is movement in the dark.)

HOLMES. *(Whispered.)* Watson?

(No reply. Stillness. **HOLMES** *moves through the room, a silhouette. He draws the shades and lights the lamp. His coat is off, discarded on a chair. His shirtsleeve is blood-soaked. He mumbles a bit as he goes about his business.)*

Solomon Moses. Solomon Moses. Incredible.

(He goes to his work table and puts a kettle on a gas burner, then takes up a clean rag and holds it to his injured arm.)

And he knew my name. Yes. He knew I would be there. How is that possible?

(And suddenly he hears someone charging up the stairs. **HOLMES** *turns, a pistol, as if by magic, in his hand. The door bursts open.)*

WATSON. Pow! Pow! Pow! Pow! Pow! Pow!

*(**WATSON** is miming shooting a pair of six-guns.* **HOLMES** *lowers the revolver quickly and pushes it down behind a chair cushion.* **WATSON** *gallops around the room like a child on a hobbyhorse.)*

Pow! Pow! Pow! Oh Holmes – you should have seen it! I thought I'd seen great horsemanship in Afghanistan when those mad Pashtuns played their wicked polo with a goat's carcass, but these fellows! The cowboys tearing along with the stampeding bison, and the magnificent Indians on their spotted ponies, flying by so close you could reach out and touch them! Absolutely cracking! Buffalo Bill himself, resplendent in his buckskins and chaps, astride his faithful old warhorse Charlie – such a striking figure. Oh, but best of all – Little Sure Shot, Queen of the Sharpshooters: Miss Annie Oakley! What a talent, Holmes! Such a lovely young woman in her fringed skirts, a pistol in each hand, standing in the stirrups and shooting glass balls out of the air as she galloped around the arena smiling all the while! Splendid! Such marksmanship! Thrilling!

HOLMES. I take it, Watson, that you are not describing dinner at your club.

WATSON. No, Holmes, of course not. Stinky Milne-Smith – you remember me speaking of Stinky. Douglas Milne-Smith. I was in hospital with him in Peshawar. Well, I bumped into Stinky in Harley Street this morning and he informed me that he had a spare ticket to the Wild West and since I had no patients in the afternoon I said yes. So I met Stinky at his club for lunch –

> *(**MRS. HUDSON** enters in her nightclothes, wearing a robe.)*

MRS. HUDSON. Gentlemen, please! Do either of you have any notion of what time it is?

WATSON. Oh…yes. Terribly sorry, Mrs. Hudson – but I thought you might still be –

> *(**HOLMES** sways on his feet. **MRS. HUDSON** sees it.)*

MRS. HUDSON. Mr. Holmes!

> *(**HOLMES** collapses into a chair, dropping the rag and revealing the blood.)*

WATSON. Holmes!

HOLMES. I'll be fine.

WATSON. Let me see –

HOLMES. Watson –

WATSON. Sherlock, let me see your arm!

HOLMES. All right.

> (**WATSON** *peels back the sleeve.* **MRS. HUDSON** *leans in to see.*)

MRS. HUDSON. Oh, good Lord!

WATSON. Hold this tightly. Mrs. Hudson, bring the lamp nearer.

> (**HOLMES** *holds the cloth as* **WATSON** *gets his bag and* **MRS. HUDSON** *brings a lamp closer.* **WATSON** *examines the wound.*)

HOLMES. He knew my name, Watson.

WATSON. Quiet.

> (**WATSON** *is now in complete control. His actions and demeanor are those a practiced battlefield surgeon, probing Holmes' arm.*)

MRS. HUDSON. Oh my. *(She looks away.)* Oh dear.

WATSON. Steady, Mrs. Hudson.

MRS. HUDSON. Yes, doctor.

WATSON. It is a nasty laceration. You're lucky. No artery has been severed. Move your fingers. Good. The tendon has been spared. But it should be seen to immediately.

> *(The kettle starts to whistle, which scares them.)*

HOLMES. I put the kettle on.

WATSON. So you did. Mrs. Hudson?

MRS. HUDSON. I'll fetch the kettle.

(She puts the lamp down and goes to get the kettle.)

WATSON. Good. Keep pressure on it.

*(While **WATSON** pulls his surgical instruments out of his bag and drops them into a shallow pan, **HOLMES** stands and paces, holding the cloth to his wound.)*

HOLMES. Solomon Moses. Immunity?

*(**WATSON** pours a glass of whiskey.)*

WATSON. I have to say I am extremely upset with you, Holmes.

HOLMES. Why?

WATSON. You know perfectly well why.

HOLMES. He knew I would be there, Watson.

WATSON. What?

HOLMES. He knew my name.

WATSON. Who? Holmes, the carpet, you're bleeding.

HOLMES. Yes, I know.

WATSON. Well, put more pressure on it, for God's sake. And sit down.

*(**HOLMES** sits. **WATSON** offers the whiskey to **HOLMES.**)*

Here.

HOLMES. I don't want any.

WATSON. Drink it.

*(**HOLMES** takes a sip. **MRS. HUDSON** returns with the steaming kettle.)*

More.

HOLMES. Yes, Doctor.

MRS. HUDSON. Here we are, Doctor.

> (**WATSON** *takes the kettle and pours the water into the pan of instruments.*)

WATSON. Thank you, Mrs. Hudson.

HOLMES. Who could offer him immunity?

MRS. HUDSON. What else can I do, Doctor?

WATSON. Well, if you feel up to it, you could hold the lamp again.

MRS. HUDSON. Of course I feel up to it.

> (**MRS. HUDSON** *drinks a small amount of whiskey.*)

> (**WATSON** *takes a probe and whatever else he needs from the pan.*)

WATSON. All right, Holmes. Try to relax.

HOLMES. The least reassuring words in the English language.

> (**WATSON** *begins cleaning the wound. It is not comfortable for* **HOLMES.**)

WATSON. More whiskey.

> (**HOLMES** *takes a healthy gulp.*)

Another.

HOLMES. Are you trying to get me drunk?

MRS. HUDSON. Drink, Sherlock.

> (**HOLMES** *takes another drink.* **WATSON** *begins dressing the wound.*)

WATSON. Is this connected with the two murders you spoke of this morning?

HOLMES. Yes, I think so.

WATSON. Why did you keep me from accompanying you tonight?

HOLMES. Believe me, Watson, I had no idea –

> (**HOLMES** *winces in pain as* **WATSON** *pours iodine into the wound.*)

WATSON. Drink.

> (**HOLMES** *does so.*)

Now, there is a bit of grit in there and it must come out.

HOLMES. Wonderful.

WATSON. You may scream but you must keep your arm still.

HOLMES. I shan't scream.

WATSON. You take too many chances, Holmes.

HOLMES. Aaaaaaahhh!

WATSON. Drink. How did this happen? I take it this is not Mr. Mark Twain's handiwork?

> (**HOLMES** *drinks.*)

HOLMES. No. There is a roiling among the criminal ranks, Watson. Some sort of realignment is taking place.

WATSON. How do you mean?

HOLMES. Since Lee Wu Chang's murder I have been watching several of London's more prominent criminals. Yesterday it was Arnold Crofters. Tonight it was Jefferson Henry, an American expatriate criminal and the leading dealer in stolen goods in the East End. As I was following him I saw his bodyguards turn on their master. There was then a murderous attack which I tried – unsuccessfully – to prevent.

WATSON. He was murdered by his bodyguards?

(**HOLMES** *nods and drinks more whiskey.*)

HOLMES. Yes. It was a trap set for both of us and I'm afraid we walked right into it.

WATSON. Do you mean they had planned to kill you?

HOLMES. Oh, yes. They very foolishly used my name – and then his; but as neither of us was meant to survive the encounter I suppose it didn't matter.

WATSON. But you knew his name.

HOLMES. What I knew, apparently, was his alias. I was told his real name just before he was murdered – Solomon Moses. Which is part of a complex of coincidences that absolutely beggars belief.

> (**WATSON** *has a sort of dressing on Holmes' arm.*)

WATSON. Do we have any clean linen, Mrs. Hudson?

MRS. HUDSON. What a thing to ask. Of course we do.

> (**MRS. HUDSON** *puts down the lamp and heads to the door.*)

WATSON. Thank you, Mrs. Hudson. (*To* **HOLMES.**) How did you escape?

HOLMES. I didn't. I was rescued.

WATSON. By whom?

HOLMES. My saviour was also an American. New York. Brooklyn most likely. Five foot ten. Twelve and a half – thirteen stone. Powerfully built. Not a policeman, I think, but...there's that blue again. Cold. Heavy like clay. Mycroft?

> (**MRS. HUDSON** *opens the door – There is a* **MAN** *standing on the threshold!*)

MRS. HUDSON. Aaaaah!

> (**HOLMES** *comes out of his chair, a pistol in his hand as* **WATSON** *whirls around at the sound of* **MRS. HUDSON** *shriek.*)

WATSON. Mrs. Hudson?

MAN. Sherlock Holmes?

MRS. HUDSON. Good Lord! Young man, you nearly scared me to death!

MAN. Sorry. Sherlock Holmes?

MRS. HUDSON. Do you have any idea what time it is?

MAN. Sherlock Holmes.

HOLMES. Mrs. Hudson –

MRS. HUDSON. Mr. Holmes is not available.

HOLMES. That's all right, Mrs. Hudson.

MRS. HUDSON. But it is nearly one o'clock in the morning!

> (**MRS. HUDSON** *has turned, revealing the men to each other.* **SHERLOCK HOLMES** *and the* **PINKERTON.** *This beggars all belief. Beat.*)

HOLMES. For this gentleman, we will make an allowance. Please come in, Mr...?

PINKS. I ain't here to visit.

MRS. HUDSON. Well, that is a relief. Dr. Watson, I appeal to you –

WATSON. Quite right, Mrs. Hudson. Yes. Of course. Thank you.

MRS. HUDSON. Gentlemen. I bid you a *good night.*

> (*She exits.* **HOLMES** *is staring at the* **PINKERTON,** *who eyes* **WATSON.**)

HOLMES. This is Dr. John Watson. He has my complete confidence.

PINKS. Good for him. *(He turns to the hall.)* You can come up now, Miss.

> *(A* **YOUNG WOMAN** *enters. She is dressed somewhat differently but she is most definitely* **MISS PHOEBE ANNE MOSES.** *Before* **HOLMES,** *who is absolutely astounded, can say anything she launches into this:)*

MOSES. Mr. Holmes, forgive me for coming here so late but I think you may be the only one who can help me.

HOLMES. The hour is of no importance, Miss –

MOSES. I did lie to you, Mr. Holmes, and I am truly sorry for that. My name is Annie Oakley.

HOLMES. I'm sorry?

WATSON. Little Sure Shot!

HOLMES. What?

WATSON. You were wonderful!

ANNIE. Pardon me?

WATSON. No, please, Miss Oakley, I beg your pardon, but I was in attendance at Earl's Court today and your performance was – in my humble opinion – the high point of an absolutely exhilarating afternoon.

ANNIE. Well, thank you –

HOLMES. Watson –

WATSON. When you galloped in at the beginning, bent down from the saddle and plucked the pistol from the ground, righted yourself and then shot those glasses – that had been tossed up in – well, I've never been so astounded in my life. Absolutely breathtaking. Holmes, you really should have been there.

HOLMES. I feel as though I was.

WATSON. And the marvelous trick-shooting with the mirror –

HOLMES. Watson!

WATSON. Yes, Holmes?

HOLMES. If I may, Miss... Oakley, this fanatic is my trusted friend and colleague Dr. John Watson.

ANNIE. Pleased to meet you, Dr. Watson, and I am so happy you liked the show.

WATSON. Oh, I did, Miss Oakley. Oh... I did.

HOLMES. Won't you sit down?

ANNIE. Thank you, Mr. Holmes but I know it's late and I don't want to take up too much of your time.

HOLMES. Still, I think you should sit.

ANNIE. All right.

(She sits.)

HOLMES. Now, Miss Oakley –

ANNIE. I want you to find out who killed my brother.

WATSON. Oh, Miss Oakley – your brother? I am so very sorry.

ANNIE. Thank you, Doctor.

PINKS. Annie, I gotta say it again – Frank wouldn't want you to be –

ANNIE. You're my bodyguard, Pinks – you do that job and leave my husband to me.

WATSON. Your husband?

ANNIE. Yes. Frank Butler. He's in Paris checking out the fairgrounds over there. He hasn't heard about it yet.

HOLMES. Pinks? Of course. You are one of Major Pinkerton's men.

ANNIE. Yes, that's why I call him "Pinks." He won't tell me his real name. But he did tell me about tonight. How did you find Solomon so quickly?

HOLMES. I didn't find him. I am loathe to admit it, Miss Oakley, but I'm afraid your brother found me.

ANNIE. Thank you for trying to save him, Mr. Holmes.

HOLMES. Why have you not gone to the police?

ANNIE. I can't. Both Colonel Cody and my husband are very much against me getting involved with my brother. They're worried about a scandal and what it might do to the show.

HOLMES. I see.

ANNIE. If we were back in the States, Pinks might be able to take care of this but he doesn't know anything about –

HOLMES. Miss Oakley –

ANNIE. I have no one else to turn to, Mr. Holmes. Won't you please help me?

    (A breath.)

HOLMES. The blue is very heavy.

ANNIE. Is that a yes, Mr. Holmes?

HOLMES. Yes. Of course I will help you, Miss Oakley.

ANNIE. Thank you, Mr. Holmes.

HOLMES. Where are you staying in London?

ANNIE. We're at the Metropole.

HOLMES. Very well. I will contact you in the next day or so.

ANNIE. If you need a hand – Pinks here can help you.

HOLMES. Yes, I know he can.

(**PINKS** *is very quietly writing a small note in the palm of his hand.*)

ANNIE. Well, come on, Pinks. *(To* **WATSON.***)* It was very nice to meet you, Dr. Watson.

WATSON. A great pleasure, Miss Oakley. And again, please accept my condolences.

ANNIE. Thank you, Doctor. I look forward to hearing from you very soon, Mr. Holmes. Good night, gentlemen. And sorry for the late visit.

(She exits. **HOLMES** *goes to* **PINKS.***)*

HOLMES. Why were you following me tonight?

PINKS. I wasn't. Why were you followin' Solomon Moses?

HOLMES. I was not. I was following Jefferson Henry because I believed he was a possible target.

PINKS. You was right.

HOLMES. You knew he was Miss Oakley's brother?

PINKS. No.

WATSON. Her brother?

HOLMES. Yes, Watson.

PINKS. Not until I heard his name.

WATSON. Moses?

HOLMES. Yes, Watson. *(To* **PINKS.***)* Then why were you following him?

PINKS. I wasn't.

WATSON. The man who tried to kill you was her brother?

HOLMES & PINKS. Yes, Watson!

WATSON. Sorry, just catching up.

HOLMES. Then whom were you following?

PINKS. The boys with the knives.

HOLMES. Why?

PINKS. Coincidence.

ANNIE. *(Offstage.)* Pinks!

HOLMES. Coincidence? Are you saying that all this –?

PINKS. I'm saying – I'll see ya.

> *(He puts out his hand, which* **HOLMES** *takes. They shake. The* **PINKS** *starts to leave.)*

HOLMES. Did you bring her to me?

PINKS. No, she brought me. Don't be late.

> *(***PINKS** *exits.)*

WATSON. Annie Oakley. Then her family name is Moses?

> *(***HOLMES** *is looking at a slip of paper given to him by* **PINKS** *as they shook hands.)*

HOLMES. Yes. Phoebe Ann Moses.

WATSON. What a thoroughly delightful young woman.

HOLMES. Extraordinary.

WATSON. Beautiful. Charming. Do you know, Holmes, she's the absolute toast of London and yet she seems completely unaffected. The best sort of American, I think.

HOLMES. Yes.

> *(The clock strikes one.)*

WATSON. Good Lord, it's one o'clock already.

HOLMES. Yes, Watson, we just have time.

> *(***HOLMES** *begins getting ready to go out. He gathers his coat, etc.)*

WATSON. Holmes, where on earth do you think you're going?

HOLMES. Whitechapel. Well, come along, Watson.

WATSON. Whitechapel? Are you mad? It is one o'clock in the morning.

HOLMES. Yes, and we must be there by two.

WATSON. Holmes, you were very nearly murdered tonight and I insist that you rest.

HOLMES. I shall rest in time, Watson. Be a good fellow and see about a cab, will you?

(**HOLMES** *throws* **WATSON** *his coat.*)

We shall need more whiskey.

(*He fills a flask.*)

WATSON. Holmes!

HOLMES. Watson, as you noted earlier today, I do not place great faith in coincidence. But I find that we are currently at a veritable nexus of coincidence. I was very nearly murdered tonight in Shadwell. This morning we were visited by Miss Charlotte Lichter, an American mining engineer whose prized invention was stolen from the St. Katherine Docks before it could be transported to Earl's Court. Earl's Court, where Annie Oakley, who has come to us tonight bearing the terrible news of her brother's murder, is performing in the Wild West and who has a private Pinkerton who just so happens to be the man who saved my life tonight in Shadwell. I hate to think that all this might be coincidence but the Pinkerton wishes to see me in Brick Lane in less than one hour and I am going to do so. Will you come with me?

WATSON. But, Holmes –

HOLMES. I am a bit weakened from loss of blood and if I must go alone –

WATSON. Oh, for God's sake! I'll get my hat.

HOLMES. Good man. And bring your revolver!

>*(WATSON grabs hat and gun and they exit.
>Lights change.)*

Scene Five

(Whitechapel. The sound of a horse-drawn hansom cab arriving and departing. **HOLMES** *and* **WATSON** *appear just as Big Ben distantly announces the hour – two a.m. They wait. The* **PINKERTON** *appears out of the shadows.)*

PINKS. Hey. You made it.

HOLMES. Of course. I am never late. Now, what brings us here?

PINKS. I got a line on the two boys we tangled with tonight. You want to run it down?

HOLMES. Yes. We will follow you.

PINKS. Okay. This way. *(They start.)* I grew up in Brooklyn. Joined the Pinks in seventy-six. I worked a slew of cases in New York. I saw a lot of faces. I did a lot of things. This job comes up, I figure – why not? Keep Annie Oakley out of trouble and see a bit of the world. The beer's fine. Everything's jake. Then I see 'em – two faces outta place.

HOLMES. American?

PINKS. Yeah. Two boys I know pretty well. Made their bones in the Points, now they run with the Whyos.

WATSON. I beg your pardon?

HOLMES. The Whyos, Watson, is an Irish-American criminal gang known to operate in and around the notorious Five Points on the island of Manhattan.

WATSON. I see. And "made their bones"?

HOLMES. To prove their worth to the gang, *(To* **PINKS.***)* they committed murder?

PINKS. Yeah.

WATSON. Good heavens.

PINKS. So, one night after the show, I tuck Annie in –

WATSON. I beg your pardon?

PINKS. Huh?

HOLMES. A figure of speech, Watson.

WATSON. Oh, I see.

PINKS. He gonna be all right?

HOLMES. He'll be fine.

WATSON. Yes, I'm fine. Carry on.

PINKS. So, I see these two boyos from back home who probably never been farther east than Coney Island and I wonder what brings 'em all the way to London – so I shadow 'em and they come to roost here.

(He points across the street.)

HOLMES. The St. George Hotel.

PINKS. Yeah. So tonight, after the show, I come back here. I wait. Then three of 'em come out. Dubby Conroy, Red Hook Boyle and a gent I never seen before.

HOLMES. Solomon Moses.

PINKS. Yeah. They get to a place – I don't know from London – some place by the river – smells like Fulton Street.

HOLMES. Shadwell.

PINKS. Okay. And that's where the Whyos moved in for the kill.

HOLMES. Why didn't you try to stop them?

PINKS. Wasn't my play. I don't know this guy from Adam. Then you stuck your nose in.

HOLMES. Why did that make a difference?

PINKS. I don't know, maybe I didn't like the odds. Two killers with pigstickers and you with a whistle.

WATSON. You shot them?

PINKS. I shot Dubby. I don't know about Red Hook.

HOLMES. Are they dead?

PINKS. I was bleedin'. I didn't wait around to find out.

HOLMES. Then who do you think is in that hotel?

PINKS. Those two boys wouldn't tie their shoes unless someone told 'em to do it.

HOLMES. You think they did not cross the ocean on their own?

PINKS. Nah, someone had to put 'em to bed and tell 'em stories.

HOLMES. And you think that someone is here?

PINKS. Could be. You want to find out who tried to kill you?

HOLMES. Yes.

WATSON. So, we wait?

PINKS. Nah, I'm tired of waitin'. You stay here. I'll see if I can flush him out.

*(The **PINKERTON** crosses towards the hotel.)*

WATSON. Who are we waiting for, Holmes? Another American criminal?

HOLMES. If the Pinkerton is correct, yes.

WATSON. Could that be the individual, the...the mastermind, you mentioned this morning?

HOLMES. Perhaps. Some whiskey, Watson?

(He offers the flask.)

WATSON. No, thank you. You shouldn't have any more, either.

HOLMES. Following doctor's orders.

WATSON. Don't blame me if you can't sleep.

HOLMES. Sleep? Are you tired, Watson? *(He sees something.)* Shush.

> *(Someone is coming out of the darkness. It is...not the* **PINKERTON.** *Decidedly not the* **PINKERTON.** *She is beautifully dressed, this woman, and she is as beautiful herself as her attire. She could not be more conspicuous on this dark, grey street than if she were a peacock in a coal mine. She is* **MRS. MARGARET MALLOY.***)*

WATSON. Good God.

HOLMES. Yes.

WATSON. What could such a fashionable young woman be doing in Whitechapel at this hour?

HOLMES. Need you ask?

WATSON. What? Oh I don't think so, Holmes. Her? No.

HOLMES. You think not?

WATSON. Well, look at her, Holmes. The poor thing might be in trouble.

HOLMES. Watson...

WATSON. She might need our help. Yes –

HOLMES. Watson, no –

> *(But* **WATSON** *strides forward bent on gallantry.* **HOLMES** *hangs back a bit.)*

WATSON. I beg your pardon –

MALLOY. Oh! Oh dear...

WATSON. I am very sorry if I frightened you, madam.

MALLOY. Oh my Lord, yes, you did give me something of a fright, sir.

WATSON. Again, my sincere apologies.

> *(She looks him over and then past him to* **HOLMES.***)*

MALLOY. That's all right. Are you –?

WATSON. My colleague and I are just waiting on an associate, you see. Is there any way in which we might be of assistance to you?

MALLOY. Oh, well, I am afraid I have lost my way, sir. I had no intention of being out at such a disgraceful hour, I assure you, but I'm afraid a friend and I had a bit of a... difference of opinion, you see and he...

WATSON. I see. Yes, of course.

MALLOY. And he...

WATSON. You do not need to explain yourself to me.

MALLOY. ...he just left me in the middle of the street!

> *(She starts to weep.)*

WATSON. The cad.

MALLOY. And I don't know London, you see and I got all turned around and I need to get to Liverpool Street Station but I... I don't have any money – oh it is so humiliating!

> *(She sobs gently into her handkerchief.)*

HOLMES. *(Quietly.)* Watson.

WATSON. *(To* **HOLMES.***)* Yes, yes, I know. *(To her.)* Now, now, you mustn't upset yourself. Please. We will help you.

MALLOY. *(Through her weeping.)* You are so kind.

WATSON. Here. Here is five pounds.

MALLOY. Oh no. No, I couldn't.

HOLMES. Watson...

WATSON. Please, you must take it. I absolutely insist. As a favor to me?

>*(She takes the note quickly and lightly like a fer-de-lance striking a mouse.)*

MALLOY. That is so wonderfully generous of you, kind sir. Thank you.

>*(She kisses him on the cheek. The **PINKERTON** enters.)*

WATSON. Oh, well. You are very welcome. Now, Liverpool Street is not far. You just follow – well, no, we should find you a cab –

>*(The **PINKERTON** sees the **WOMAN**'s face.)*

PINKS. Christ! Maggie!

>*(The **WOMAN** sees **PINKS**.)*

MALLOY. Well, I'll be buggered!

WATSON. I beg your –

PINKS. Get away from her!

MALLOY. You sonofabitch!

>*(The **WOMAN** pushes **WATSON** out of the way and reaches under her dress as the **PINKS** reaches for his gun.)*

HOLMES. Mr. Pinks!

>*(The **WOMAN** pulls a knife from her boot and throws it at the **PINKERTON**, who leans out its path as it passes him and then thunks into the wall. The **WOMAN** turns and runs away.*

The **PINKERTON** *runs after her.* **HOLMES** *and*
WATSON *are left standing in amazement.)*

I daresay that is five pounds you will never see again.

WATSON. But, Holmes –

HOLMES. Well, come, Watson, the game – quite obviously –
is afoot!

> *(They run off after the* **PINKS** *and the*
> **WOMAN.** *There is now a chase through the*
> *streets of London. From Whitechapel to*
> *Cannon Street, past St Paul's, Fleet Street,*
> *the Strand, to the Embankment and south of*
> *the Houses of Parliament. Or whatever route*
> *offers the greatest opportunity for thrills.*
> *The* **MEN** *follow her together and possibly*
> *split up as various obstacles are presented*
> *to them: drunken revelers of both high and*
> *low society; descents into tunnels beneath*
> *the streets and then up again; a chase and*
> *a fight across the tops of moving rail cars.*
> *Whatever is at hand, the more creative the*
> *better. Ultimately* **MAGGIE MALLOY** *– for*
> *that is her name – escapes their pursuit. The*
> **PINKERTON, HOLMES,** *and* **WATSON** *arrive*
> *just as she disappears.)*

PINKS. Goddammit!

WATSON. My God, what a woman!

HOLMES. Who is she?

PINKS. It's "Mayhem."

WATSON. I beg your pardon?

PINKS. "Mayhem" Maggie Malloy.

HOLMES. A dangerous woman, is she?

PINKS. There's no one more dangerous, man or woman.

WATSON. Extraordinary.

PINKS. Hey – is there a boat around here? Some kind of horse ferry?

HOLMES. Horseferry?

PINKS. Yeah, she said somethin' about a horse ferry to that yard boss back there.

HOLMES. Well done, detective.

WATSON. Horseferry Road?

HOLMES. Yes, she's on her way to Pimlico! Come along, gentlemen, we may just have time.

>*(They rush off as we continue our transition to: Horseferry Road. We are near the river just west of Lambeth Bridge. MAGGIE MALLOY enters. She is confident that she has lost her pursuers and makes her way to a spot that allows for some cover. She lights a cigarette and waits.)*
>
>*(During the final part of the transition a large collection of wooden crates is revealed as part of the scene.)*
>
>*(HOLMES, PINKS, and WATSON creep in from the shadows. They see MAGGIE and position themselves to wait. A certain amount of gestural communication may be allowed. Then MAGGIE sees something.)*
>
>*(A MAN has appeared: middle-aged with grey hair. He is well dressed in a slightly formal, somber fashion. This is MAJOR RAMSEY. He is unhurried as he makes his way down the road, apparently unaware of the woman who is waiting for him.)*
>
>*(They watch as the grey-haired man stops when confronted by MAGGIE MALLOY.*

MALLOY appears to be speaking to the older man. Is she pulling the same scam on him that she did on Watson? The man reaches into his inside breast pocket, but before he can bring his hand out.)

HOLMES. Mrs. Malloy!

(For a moment everything is still.)

RAMSEY. What is the meaning of this?

HOLMES. We have no interest in harming you.

(MALLOY turns and sees PINKS.)

MALLOY. Well... Hello Pinky.

PINKS. Hello, Margaret.

MALLOY. Oh, so formal for such an old friend. You be honest with me, now, sweetheart – was it you that shot my boys?

PINKS. Yeah, it was me, Maggie. Like all your men – you shoulda taken better care of 'em.

MALLOY. Oh? Well, maybe you're right. Speakin' of men not taken care of – how's your little brother?

(PINKS tenses.)

PINKS. He's just fine, Maggie. How's Mr. Malloy?

MALLOY. You...goddamn...lousy...two-timin' –

PINKS. What are you doin' here, Maggie?

MALLOY. Well, I'll tell you, shamus; first I'm gonna kill this little shitheel, and then I'm goin' to kill you!

(Just as MAGGIE and PINKS are raising their guns ANNIE OAKLEY appears and fires two shots from her pistol. MAGGIE screams, grabs her hand and drops her revolver while the gun flies out of PINKS' hand. RAMSEY falls to

> *the ground as if in a faint. There is a moment*
> *of stunned immobility and then.)*

You're mine, flatfoot!

> (**MAGGIE** *throws a knife at the* **PINKS,** *who*
> *ducks and the knife is caught by* **ANNIE.**
> **MAGGIE** *rushes off into the night.)*

ANNIE. Mr. Holmes! We need to talk!

WATSON. Miss Oakley!

PINKS. Annie, what the hell are you doin' here?

ANNIE. My husband's outta town and I'm lookin' for a little fun! What do you think?

HOLMES. Watson, your assistance, please.

> (**HOLMES** *and* **WATSON** *see to the man on the*
> *ground.)*

PINKS. You know you shouldn't –

ANNIE. My brother was murdered tonight and I am in this now whether you like it or not!

PINKS. You know for a fact that Frank doesn't want you getting involved in any of this.

ANNIE. You let me worry about what my husband wants and doesn't want, okay?

PINKS. Goddammit!

ANNIE. And watch your language!

WATSON. Remarkable.

RAMSEY. *(Seated on the ground.)* Are you the police?

HOLMES. No. My name is Sherlock Holmes. I am a consulting detective. This is Dr. John Watson. That gentleman is...an American operative and the young lady is Miss Annie Oakley.

RAMSEY. Little Sure Shot!

ANNIE. Hello, there, sir. Are you all right?

RAMSEY. Yes, thank you. Yes, I thank you all for your assistance, I assure you. Most helpful.

(He sits up.)

WATSON. We should see you to hospital.

RAMSEY. No, no, I am quite well, thank you. Just a bit of a shock, you know.

(With some assistance he gets to his feet.)

Thank you. Thank you. Oh. Now, I really must be on my way.

HOLMES. Sir, if I may ask: why should that woman have wanted to kill you?

RAMSEY. Kill me? Oh no, no, I'm quite certain that her intent was simply to rob me. Which is shocking, enough, I assure you. She seemed so...so vulnerable at first. She said that she was lost and would I help her. I suppose it is foolish of me to walk alone at such an hour but I am afraid that I have grown very fond of my nocturnal rambles. Now, I really must be getting back to my rooms.

HOLMES. Pardon me, but, Mr...?

RAMSEY. Ramsey is my name. Major T.I. Ramsey.

HOLMES. T.I.?

RAMSEY. Yes. Thaddeus Isaac. Thanks to my dear mother. Well, gentleman. And Miss... Oakley? I am very much in your debt. Thank you. Thank you all. *(He starts off.)* Oh dear. Such a night.

(He exits.)

HOLMES. Major T.I. Ramsey.

PINKS. Ring any bells?

HOLMES. No, nothing immediately comes to mind.

ANNIE. Mr. Holmes, do you think that woman had something to do with Solomon's murder?

> (**WATSON** *is standing by the wall of wooden crates.*)

HOLMES. Miss Oakley, if you truly want my assistance / in this matter –

WATSON. Holmes.

HOLMES. Just a moment, Watson. *(To* ANNIE.*)* You must allow me to work / without any interference –

WATSON. Holmes!

HOLMES. Yes, Watson, what is it?

WATSON. Here. Look here.

> (**HOLMES** *goes to him. He looks at the stenciling on one of the larger crates.*)

HOLMES. C.C. Lichter, American Exhibition, Earl's Court, London.

WATSON. It is Charlotte Lichter's Mechanical Mole!

HOLMES. Oh, now, this really is too much.

> (*Music*. Lights fade to black.*)

End of Act I

ACT II

Scene One

(Baker Street, the afternoon of that same day. **WATSON** *is changing the dressing on Holmes' arm as* **HOLMES** *goes about his business, which includes the reading and writing of telegrams.)*

HOLMES. Mrs. Hudson!

WATSON. Hold still, for Heaven's sake.

HOLMES. Mrs. Hudson!

HUDSON. *(Offstage.)* Coming, Mr. Holmes.

WATSON. You are the worst patient in the world.

HOLMES. I am sorry, Watson, but I haven't the time – Mrs. Hudson!

HUDSON. *(Offstage.)* Just there, Mr. Holmes, just there!

> *(**MRS. HUDSON** enters with a coffee pot and a handful of telegrams.)*

More telegrams for you, Mr. Holmes.

HOLMES. Capital. Have the boy take these out immediately.

> *(He offers her three telegram forms.)*

HUDSON. Very well.

(She places the coffee pot on the table, takes the telegrams from **HOLMES** *and picks up the empty pot.)*

HOLMES. *(Reading telegram.)* And more coffee, if you please.

(She shares a wry look with **WATSON** *as she leaves.* **WATSON** *is closing up his medical bag. He pours more coffee.)*

WATSON. What news?

HOLMES. From Inspector Gregson. As we suspected, Miss Lichter's crates were all empty. No evidence of where the Mole may be. Remarkable.

*(***HOLMES*** picks up a small glass bottle with what looks like red dust in it.)*

WATSON. Why remarkable?

HOLMES. Twenty-three hardwood crates containing five tons of excavating equipment are stolen from the St. Katherine Docks. Less than forty-eight hours later they are found – empty – in Horseferry Road, fully three miles from where they were stolen. Found by the very man hired to find them, even though – at the time – I was not actually looking for them.

WATSON. Another coincidence?

HOLMES. I pray not.

(He opens a second telegram.)

And as for Mrs. Malloy – where is she hiding?

*(***ANNIE OAKLEY*** *and the* ***PINKS*** *are speaking as they enter the room.)*

ANNIE. Oh, stop mopin' around, Pinks.

PINKS. I ain't mopin!

ANNIE. Good morning, gentlemen.

WATSON. Good morning, Miss Oakley.

PINKS. Your landlady says you've got coffee up here.

HOLMES. Of course. Allow me.

*(***HOLMES*** pours ***PINKS*** a cup of coffee.)*

WATSON. How are you this morning, Miss Oakley?

ANNIE. I'm fine, Dr. Watson. Thank you for asking.

WATSON. Would you care for some coffee?

ANNIE. Not just now, thanks. Good morning Mr. Holmes.

HOLMES. Miss Oakley.

*(***PINKS*** sits down and grimaces.)*

WATSON. Is your arm bothering you?

PINKS. I got shot. That bothers me. *(To ***HOLMES.****)* You call this coffee?

HOLMES. Not strong enough for you?

WATSON. *(Re: shoulder.)* Let me see it.

PINKS. It's good, thanks.

HOLMES. I can have Mrs. Hudson make a stronger pot.

*(***WATSON*** retrieves his medical bag.)*

PINKS. *(Re: coffee.)* Nah, it's fine.

WATSON. I should look at your wound.

PINKS. No you shouldn't.

WATSON. You will please take off your jacket and shirt.

PINKS. Look, it's fine. I had the doc with the show take a look at it.

WATSON. You have a surgeon with the Wild West?

PINKS. Yeah. He looks after everybody – the horses, them buffalo –

HOLMES. Bison.

PINKS. – everybody.

WATSON. A veterinarian?

ANNIE. Oh, Pinks, you had Doc Carter sew you up?

WATSON. You had a veterinarian see to your bullet wound?

PINKS. Hey, he's seen plenty of bullet holes, don't you worry.

ANNIE. He's a drunk, Pinks.

PINKS. So?

WATSON. My good man, if the wound becomes septic –

PINKS. Let it go, doc!

> (**HOLMES** *retrieves an envelope from the bureau.*)

WATSON. As you wish. But you may require my services later.

PINKS. Why?

WATSON. Because I have a good deal of experience with amputation.

PINKS. Thanks, doc. I'll keep that in mind.

HOLMES. Here you are, Miss Oakley.

> (*He offers her an envelope.*)

ANNIE. What is it?

HOLMES. Your cheque.

ANNIE. No, Mr. Holmes.

HOLMES. It is entirely possible that the two men who stabbed your brother are dead.

ANNIE. I know. Pinks got 'em.

HOLMES. Yes. Perhaps you should give this to him.

ANNIE. Do you believe those men planned my brother's murder?

HOLMES. No.

ANNIE. Do you know who did?

HOLMES. Not yet.

ANNIE. Then please keep that check until you do.

HOLMES. If you insist.

ANNIE. Thank you.

(**HOLMES** *opens a third telegram.*)

PINKS. So what's on the plate for today?

WATSON. You really should rest, you know. A bullet wound is nothing to be –

PINKS. Thanks, doc, but I already got a mother.

ANNIE. Pinks!

HOLMES. Well, well.

WATSON. What is it?

HOLMES. It seems there is a Major Ramsey in London.

WATSON. Aha!

HOLMES. But we have yet to locate him.

WATSON. I have to say, Holmes, this Ramsey seemed rather unassuming.

HOLMES. He was targeted for a reason, Watson –

WATSON. Yes, but do you really think that a man as docile as this Major Ramsey could be the head of some criminal conspiracy?

HOLMES. – and despite what he may claim, that reason was not robbery.

PINKS. I'm not sure about that. Maggie Malloy is not above robbin' an old man for a few bucks.

WATSON. Yes, Holmes, this "Mayhem" strikes me as a much more viable candidate for criminal mastermind.

HOLMES. No, it cannot be her.

ANNIE. Why? Because she's an American?

HOLMES. Oh, please, Miss Oakley –

ANNIE. Or because she's a woman?

HOLMES. Because she is...not right.

WATSON. Holmes –

ANNIE. Not right?

PINKS. Hey look, I know Maggie Malloy. She's as crooked as they come, she's plenty smart and she's not afraid of anyone.

HOLMES. That's not the point –

WATSON. But Holmes, doesn't it seem obvious that Mrs. Malloy came to London with the other Whyos in order to execute some sort of coup d'etat in the underworld?

PINKS.	**ANNIE.**
She could do it!	She might have killed my brother!

(HOLMES loses it.)

HOLMES. For God's sake you are just saying words!

(He tries to gather himself as the others just stare. He holds up a telegram.)

All right. Mrs. Malloy. It should be no great surprise that she is no longer residing at the St. George Hotel. Mr. Pinks, might you be able to locate her?

PINKS. Yeah. Yeah, I can do that.

HOLMES. Good. According to this telegram she has not been seen there since last night.

PINKS. Wednesday. Okay, I'll run it down.

ANNIE. We'll run it down.

PINKS. No, Annie.

ANNIE. I've got a few hours before I have to / be at the show, Pinks.

PINKS. You know what Frank would / say

ANNIE. My husband would say you're my bodyguard, Pinks, and you can't guard my body if you're flatfootin' it all over London without me.

PINKS. All right! So, gents, see ya back here?

HOLMES. Yes. Shall we say ten o'clock?

PINKS. See ya then. *(To* **ANNIE.***)* Well, c'mon if you're coming.

> *(He exits.)*

ANNIE. Thank you for the hospitality, Doctor. Mr. Holmes – find the man – *or the woman* – who killed my brother.

> *(***ANNIE** *exits.)*

WATSON. Holmes, I am not going into the office – today is Thursday!

HOLMES. Brilliant, Watson. And if I follow your reasoning will tomorrow be Friday?

WATSON. Very funny. No, I mean tonight. Thursday. The Rothchilds.

HOLMES. Yes, I know. Uncle Emile.

WATSON. That's right. Nine o'clock.

HOLMES. Mrs. Hudson!

WATSON. If we are unable to attend, we should get word to Mycroft.

HOLMES. I'll see to it.

(**MRS. HUDSON** *enters with more coffee and a piece of note paper.*)

Mrs. Hudson!

HUDSON. I'm not deaf yet, Mr. Holmes.

HOLMES. Have any more –

HUDSON. One more telegram for you.

(*She hands him the telegram.*)

HOLMES. Ah. Capital.

WATSON. Thank you, Mrs. Hudson.

(*She exits.*)

HOLMES. We may have found our mystery man, Watson.

WATSON. This Major Ramsey?

HOLMES. Yes. It seems his rooms are in Lambeth.

WATSON. Which is not far from where we saw him last night.

HOLMES. And apparently he makes his living as an Army tutor.

WATSON. Well, that would make sense. If he had been an officer.

HOLMES. Did he strike you as a military man?

WATSON. Well, perhaps not in any obvious way –

HOLMES. For good reason, Watson: he isn't.

(**HOLMES** *grabs his coat and hat.* **WATSON** *begins to do the same.*)

WATSON. Holmes – all right, then. Where are we going? Lambeth?

HOLMES. That is where I am headed. You, however, must –

WATSON. I'm going with you.

HOLMES. No, Watson.

WATSON. Holmes, you refused my help yesterday and you were very nearly murdered.

HOLMES. Yes, I know, but it's broad daylight, Watson, and you have seen this man – docile, unassuming – he is no threat to me.

WATSON. You are doing it again, Holmes.

HOLMES. Whatever do you mean?

WATSON. Placing yourself in harm's way / for no good reason.

HOLMES. Watson –

WATSON. No, I am going to say this, Holmes – you know as well as I that when you are not working, when you have no case to occupy your mind, you often distract yourself and *seriously jeopardize your health* with the use of morphine and cocaine.

HOLMES. Watson, please –

WATSON. But when you are working you just as often expose yourself to other unnecessary dangers. I have to wonder sometimes if you don't have some sort of death wish –

HOLMES. Don't be ridiculous!

WATSON. Now you're going off half-cocked to terrorize some helpless old man.

HOLMES. Watson!

WATSON. I insist that you let me help you.

HOLMES. Then help me!

> *(A beat.)*

WATSON. Holmes.

> (**HOLMES** *holds up the small glass jar with the reddish dirt.*)

HOLMES. It is crucial that you discover exactly where this clay originated.

WATSON. Clay? Holmes, please, you must –

HOLMES. I found it adhered to some of Miss Lichter's crates. It is unique to one area of London. This clay is why there were brickworks near Westminster in Roman times.

WATSON. But Holmes –

HOLMES. I thank you for your concern, John, truly I do. But this is critical.

WATSON. Very well.

> (**HOLMES** *gathers their coats, hats, etc.*)

HOLMES. Now, you must look for any large excavations in an area bordered on the west by Sloane Street, on the south and east by the river, and no farther north than say... Green Park.

> (**WATSON** *is putting on his coat, hat, etc.*)

WATSON. But what is the significance of the clay?

HOLMES. Watson, what is the mole's natural milieu?

WATSON. Underground.

HOLMES. Precisely! You must find where Charlotte Lichter's Mole has gone to ground!

> *(They exit. As the transition out of Baker Street begins:)*

> *(Upstage: We see* **MAGGIE MALLOY** *leading the* **AMERICAN AMBASSADOR** *by his one good arm. She is whispering into his ear. He is smiling. He is thrilled. She laughs. They exit still in close conference as we complete the transition to:)*

Scene Two

(Shabby rooms in Lambeth. A sort of high garret office. A writing table and two chairs. A tea service is on the table. A small window as if in a gable-end dormer is upstage. **MAJOR T. I. RAMSEY** *is standing on his chair, dropping bread crumbs through a tiny opening in the dirty little window. Outside we hear the cooing of pigeons. Then we hear a bell ring as if a downstairs door has been opened and closed.* **MAJOR RAMSEY** *turns to see* **SHERLOCK HOLMES** *walking up the stairs to his little garret.* **HOLMES** *stops on the landing beneath the little room.)*

RAMSEY. Oh.

HOLMES. Good afternoon, sir.

RAMSEY. Is it... Mr. Holmes?

HOLMES. Yes. Forgive me for calling on you unannounced.

RAMSEY. Oh, well, nothing to be forgiven, I assure you. Won't you come up?

HOLMES. Thank you.

*(**HOLMES** walks up the last few stairs to the little office as **RAMSEY** gets down from the chair.)*

Do you keep pigeons, sir?

RAMSEY. I suppose in a way I do. Quite informally, I think.

HOLMES. Have you given any of them names?

RAMSEY. Yes. I confess that I have named one or two of them.

HOLMES. Then I am afraid you keep pigeons.

RAMSEY. Yes, I am afraid you are correct. *(They share a small laugh)* Please, do sit down.

HOLMES. Thank you.

> *(They sit.* **RAMSEY** *begins to pour a cup of tea.)*

RAMSEY. I am just having my tea. Will you have some?

HOLMES. No, thank you.

RAMSEY. However did you find me?

HOLMES. As I think I mentioned to you last night, sir, I make my living as a consulting detective.

RAMSEY. Oh, yes, of course...yes. Tell me if you will, has it then become natural for you to, to...ferret things out?

HOLMES. Yes, I suppose it has.

RAMSEY. Remarkable. You're quite sure you won't have some tea? The biscuits are excellent.

HOLMES. Thank you, but I took a rather late breakfast.

RAMSEY. Of course. Because of your late night, you have had a late morning. How is that for deduction, eh?

HOLMES. Very good, sir. And what of your late night? Any ill effects from your assault?

RAMSEY. How kind of you to ask, Mr. Holmes. Strangely enough, my neck pains me. I don't know why. But for *that* the entire experience might have been some dreadful dream.

HOLMES. All too real, I'm afraid.

RAMSEY. Yes, my neck concurs with you.

> *(A brief beat.)*

Is that the reason for this...delightful visit?

HOLMES. Your neck?

RAMSEY. My condition.

HOLMES. I was concerned, yes.

RAMSEY. Your concern for a stranger's wellbeing is touching, Mr. Holmes. The biscuits are very good, I assure you. They're my favorites. The ginger biscuits from *Barnes and Finlay*. Purchased for me by a student earlier today. Are you sure you won't have one?

HOLMES. Perhaps I will have just one, thank you.

(**HOLMES** *takes a biscuit.*)

RAMSEY. Excellent. And then you must have some tea as well.

HOLMES. If you insist.

RAMSEY. I certainly do. There we are.

(*He hands* **HOLMES** *a cup of tea.*)

HOLMES. Splendid.

RAMSEY. I'm sure that your life as a detective must be fascinating, Mr. Holmes. I should love, someday, to hear all about your / adventures, but –

HOLMES. There have been three murders so far.

RAMSEY. I beg your pardon?

HOLMES. Lee Wu Chang. Arnold Crofters. Solomon Moses.

RAMSEY. And who were these gentlemen?

HOLMES. They were all prominent members of the London criminal class.

RAMSEY. Oh my. And you say they were murdered?

HOLMES. Yes. All in the last two weeks.

RAMSEY. Heavens. Do you have any notion as to why they were killed?

HOLMES. I believe a war is being waged for control of the entire London underworld.

RAMSEY.   Dear me. You make it sound as if crime in London is...is organized.

HOLMES. Yes.

RAMSEY. Are you quite sure that such an organization exists?

HOLMES. I believe that such an organization is in the process of being created.

RAMSEY. Really?

HOLMES. I am equally certain that behind this process lies a single organizing intellect.

RAMSEY. You think an individual is responsible?

HOLMES. I believe so, yes.

RAMSEY. Fascinating.

HOLMES. You make your living as an Army tutor?

RAMSEY. Hmm?

HOLMES. You're an Army tutor, Mr...?

RAMSEY.   Ramsey. Major Ramsey. Yes, and as I am expecting a Captain Fleming at half-past –

HOLMES. No.

RAMSEY. I beg your pardon?

HOLMES. Forgive me, sir, but you are not Major Ramsey.

RAMSEY. No?

HOLMES. No.

(Beat.)

RAMSEY. Well, if I am not who I say I am, who am I?

HOLMES. I do not yet know your name, sir. But I shall.

RAMSEY. Mr. Holmes, please –

HOLMES. And though I may not know who you are, sir, I believe I know what you are.

RAMSEY. Mr. Holmes, I really have no idea / what you mean –

HOLMES. Your speech tells me that you are an educated man. The pin in your cravat is from Trinity College, Oxford. The slight flattening of your long vowels indicates that you have spent some considerable time in the northeast – Yorkshire, perhaps, but I think more likely, Durham? The University there, I should say. Yes. Your posture – the slumped shoulders and concave thorax – would suggest a life spent seated, reading, figuring. Your hands are very soft but you have a pronounced callous on your right index finger that indicates the chronic use of a slide rule. You may be an engineer – or possibly an astronomer – although the physical evidence of a sedentary life would lead me to propose that you are a mathematician. Now, a Trinity man who taught mathematics at Durham shouldn't be difficult to track down.

RAMSEY. Oh!

HOLMES. I beg your pardon?

RAMSEY. I've lost my biscuit in my tea.

HOLMES. Last night, sir, during your encounter with Mrs. Malloy –

RAMSEY. Oh, was that that dreadful woman's name?

HOLMES. – you reached into your inside breast pocket. What was it that you had there?

RAMSEY. Mr. Holmes. Please. You are a consulting detective? You are unofficial, then. An adjunct to the police, but not the police.

HOLMES. Was it money to pay Mrs. Malloy for her deadly services?

RAMSEY. While pursuing your inquiries, then, you do not possess the true power of the law.

HOLMES. Or perhaps it was a pistol to close out her account altogether?

RAMSEY. And apparently neither are you bound by the law's many strictures.

HOLMES. What did you have there in your pocket, Mister... or is it Doctor?

RAMSEY. Mr. Holmes, you really must stop!

HOLMES. I'm sorry, have I frightened you, Doctor? Or might it be... *Professor*?

RAMSEY. It is Major! Major Ramsey.

(The bell at the door rings. RAMSEY stands.)

That will be Captain Fleming.

HOLMES. Are you quite sure?

RAMSEY. Please do not think for a moment that I have not thoroughly enjoyed our little interview when I say I earnestly hope that this will be the last time that I have the pleasure of your company.

HOLMES. Regardless of your heartfelt denials, sir, I believe you tried to have me killed last night.

*(A **YOUNG OFFICER** appears on the stairs.)*

FLEMING. Major Ramsey – is everything all right?

RAMSEY. Yes, Captain Fleming. This gentleman was just leaving. Good bye, Mr. Holmes.

*(**HOLMES** takes another biscuit from the plate.)*

HOLMES. Thank you for the biscuits.

*(He exits. **RAMSEY** and **FLEMING** look after him.)*

(In the transition we see **WATSON**, *lantern in hand, coming out of the darkness of a tunnel. He has found what he was looking for – the red clay.)*

WATSON.   That's it. Finally. I found it. This is where the Mechanical Mole must have begun its descent. Amazing. Oh, damn. A perfectly good pair of boots ruined. But all in a good cause. Right.

*(***WATSON*** pockets the sample of clay and goes on his way.)*

(Then – as we continue to transition back into Baker Street – we see **HOLMES** *standing on Lambeth Bridge, looking out over the river. He is ruminating on the case. He nibbles at the biscuit.)*

HOLMES.   The killings in the east. The theft of the Mole. But the clay from the crates...the crates. The Mole – what? Along the river? A barge? The tremors – an earthquake in the west. Obviously. But why?

(He takes another bite of the biscuit.)

What is that? Ginger, yes. But almost a hint of licorice? Good God! It can't be. No. Yes. That's it. It must be. Biscuits!

(Ideally we have almost no transition into:)

Scene Three

(Baker Street. About eight o'clock that evening.
HOLMES *comes tearing into his rooms.)*

HOLMES. Mrs. Hudson! Mrs. Hudson!

MRS. HUDSON. *(Offstage.)* Yes, Mr. Holmes, I'm coming!

> *(***HOLMES*** *has started rummaging through a*
> *pile of newspapers.)*

HOLMES. Mrs. Hudson!

> *(***MRS. HUDSON*** *enters, with a tray and a*
> *dinner service, which she begins to place on*
> *the table.)*

MRS. HUDSON. Yes, Mr. Holmes, your supper is just on
its –

HOLMES. Mrs. Hudson; *Barnes and Finlay*, the bakeshop
in Victoria Street –

MRS. HUDSON. Actually, they're on Carlisle Place, Mr.
Holmes.

HOLMES. You shop there frequently, don't you?

MRS. HUDSON. I wouldn't say frequently, Mr. Holmes. I
try to bake fresh as much as possible, but their ginger
biscuits are just –

HOLMES. Yes, yes, their biscuits are sublime, but is not
Barnes and Finlay also famous for being closed one
day of the week?

MRS. HUDSON. Oh, yes. They're closed Thursdays.

> *(***HOLMES*** *stops rummaging.)*

HOLMES. Thursdays?

MRS. HUDSON. Yes. I've always supposed it was because
they're open all the day Saturday.

HOLMES. Today is Thursday.

MRS. HUDSON. Yes. But I've baked some lovely scones today and there's bread in the oven.

HOLMES. Thursday!

(He starts rummaging again.)

MRS. HUDSON. Will you be wanting your supper now?

HOLMES. Sorry?

MRS. HUDSON. Your supper?

(He finds the paper he's looking for.)

HOLMES. No, I don't think we shall have time for supper, Mrs. Hudson. It's Thursday! But coffee would be much appreciated I assure you.

MRS. HUDSON. Oh. Very well.

(MRS. HUDSON is just leaving as WATSON enters.)

WATSON. Holmes!

MRS. HUDSON. Good evening, Doctor.

WATSON. Hello, Mrs. Hudson.

MRS. HUDSON. No supper for you, apparently.

WATSON. Oh?

MRS. HUDSON. No, it's Thursday.

WATSON. I'm sorry?

HOLMES. *(The newspaper.)* Here it is!

WATSON. I've got it, Holmes!

HOLMES. So have I.

WATSON. What?

HOLMES. I'm sorry, Watson. What have you got?

WATSON. The red clay. You were right. There is a new excavation, east of Victoria, just off Francis Street by the Post Office. And it is precisely the same material – you see – it's identical.

(He shows **HOLMES** *the two samples.)*

HOLMES. Yes, I see. Victoria? Well done, Watson.

*(***MRS. HUDSON** *re-enters with coffee.)*

MRS. HUDSON. Your coffee, gentlemen. And a few scones.

WATSON. Oh, thank you, Mrs. Hudson.

HOLMES. Here. Yes! Victoria Street –

MRS. HUDSON. Carlisle Place.

HOLMES. *What are they up to?*

*(***WATSON** *eats a scone, sips coffee.* **MRS. HUDSON** *exits.)*

WATSON. What is who up to?

HOLMES. *What would they be after?*

WATSON. Holmes, who are you talking about? This Malloy woman?

HOLMES. Perhaps.

WATSON. The man in Lambeth?

HOLMES. Yes, Watson. He gave me a biscuit.

WATSON. A biscuit?

HOLMES. Yes. A ginger biscuit. Purchased from *Barnes and Finlay.* Today. Thursday.

WATSON. Seems a long way to go – all the way from Lambeth to Pimlico for biscuits. Ginger or not. Holmes –

HOLMES. Here, Watson. Yesterday's paper.

WATSON. *(Reading.)* "A series of small earthquakes centered near Victoria Street rumbled through Westminster yesterday morning" – of course! The Mechanical Mole was the source of those tremors.

HOLMES. Yes, Watson. Charlotte Lichter's Mole arrived at the St. Katherine Docks on the thirty-first. Two weeks later the ground shakes in Westminster and on that same day Arnold Crofters, of the Bank of England, is found stabbed to death in Whitechapel.

WATSON. Holmes, I've been meaning to ask: I don't suppose this Crofters, the bank clerk, might have had something to do with the gas explosion?

HOLMES. What gas explosion?

WATSON. You remember. A fortnight ago. In Cheapside.

HOLMES. An explosion in Cheapside? Near the Bank?

WATSON. *In* the Bank, I think.

> *(Another piece of the puzzle slides into place for* **HOLMES.***)*

HOLMES. A fortnight ago.

WATSON. Yes.

HOLMES. A fortnight ago: Lee Wu Chang was stabbed to death. The Mechanical Mole arrived in London. There is an explosion in – The Bank of England…an explosion in the Bank. Good Lord!

WATSON. What is it?

HOLMES. Dynamite!

WATSON. What?

HOLMES. They took something!

WATSON. Who?

HOLMES. Solomon Moses! He was an explosives engineer in Grant's Army. Yes. *The American!* Of course, that is why he had the pipe!

WATSON. Who?

HOLMES. Where is the Gazetteer?

WATSON.   Above the Britannica, I think, between Bullfinch's and the Bible.

> *(**HOLMES** grabs a book from the shelf and starts leafing through it.)*

HOLMES. Oh, Watson, I believe you may have done it again.

WATSON. Done what?

HOLMES. Stumbled onto the truth.

WATSON. Stumbled?

HOLMES. Yes! Because situated in Victoria Street, beneath which the earthquake rumbled and just around the corner from Carlisle Place lies – the American Embassy!

> *(**MRS. HUDSON** returns with a tray to begin clearing the table.)*

WATSON. The American Embassy?

MRS. HUDSON. In Victoria Street?

HOLMES. Yes. They brought the Mole to Francis Street and began to tunnel. Now, from the new excavation near the Post Office at Francis Street...

WATSON. I discovered it.

MRS. HUDSON. Oh?

HOLMES. ...to *Barnes and Finlay* of the famous ginger biscuits at Carlisle Place...

WATSON. Well, I stumbled onto it, apparently.

MRS. HUDSON. I see.

HOLMES. ...to the American Embassy in Victoria Street. It is, of course, a straight line. For God's sake!

WATSON. What is it, Holmes?

HOLMES. Mycroft!

WATSON. What?

HOLMES. That is why Solomon Moses thought he had immunity. Watson! It's all yellow!

WATSON. Oh dear.

MRS. HUDSON. What is it, Doctor?

WATSON. *(Whispered.)* Yellow usually signifies danger, I think.

MRS. HUDSON. I see.

HOLMES. What did he say, Watson? He said something.

WATSON. Who? When?

HOLMES. Yesterday morning, when he left here, Mycroft was at the door – he said something – what was it?

WATSON. He said...he said, "Remember, Sherlock: For Mother – Don't be late."

HOLMES. Those were his exact words? He said "Don't be late"?

WATSON. Yes, I think so.

HOLMES. I am never late. Come, Watson. There is no time to lose.

      (**HOLMES** *starts collecting his things.*)

WATSON. But Holmes what –

HOLMES. As you so trenchantly observed earlier, Watson, today is Thursday. *Barnes and Finlay* – the bakers in Carlisle Place, just around the corner from the American Embassy – is closed on Thursdays. Our mystery man – the Army tutor – had ginger biscuits purchased today from *Barnes and Finlay*. Mycroft, my brother who would much prefer having his fingernails pulled out to attending a large social function has invited us to just such a gathering on this, Thursday evening. And now, "For Mother: Don't be late." And although that is completely distinct from *Thursdays*, which shimmer like herring in a dark sea, it floats along as a kind of yellow smoke and it tastes of licorice. Come along!

WATSON. But where are we going?

HOLMES. You know precisely where you are going, Watson! *(He tosses the vial of red clay to* **WATSON.***)* You found it. You did not stumble onto it. Bring your revolver!

> *(***HOLMES** *rushes through the door.)*

WATSON. But Holmes!

HOLMES. I'm counting on you, John!

> *(And he is gone.* **WATSON** *rushes to put on his coat and grab his hat and pistol.)*

WATSON. Holmes! Damn it, Holmes. You're going to get yourself killed!

MRS. HUDSON. Oh dear!

> *(He pauses at the door, looks at the vial of clay.)*

WATSON. Right!

> *(***WATSON** *rushes from the room.)*

MRS. HUDSON. Yellow?

(*Music**. *As we begin this transition we see* **HOLMES** *on his way and The* **PINKERTON** *shadowing him.* **ANNIE OAKLEY** *is following the* **PINKERTON**.)

---

* A license to produce *Sherlock Holmes and The American Problem* does not include a performance license for any third-party or copyrighted music. Licensees should create an original composition or use music in the public domain. For further information, please see the Music and Third Party Materials Use Note on page iii.

Scene Four

(Darkness. Distant sounds of the city. Upstage we see windows dimly lit by the gaslight from the street beyond. Barnes and Finlay can be seen in large commercial script, written backwards across the window. Occasionally the shadows of a few pedestrians can be seen walking on the street outside. Quiet. Then a trapdoor opens in the floor and a shaft of dim light shines up from the opening. Someone climbs up a ladder from below and soon we see that it is **MAGGIE MALLOY***. She has a lantern and after getting out of the trap speaks in a harsh whisper to someone below her.)*

MALLOY. C'mon, Red Hook, give it here.

BOYLE. Well, give us a hand, will ya?

MALLOY. If you and your idiot partner hadn't let that sonofabitch from Flatbush get the drop on you you'd of had someone else to help you up the ladder you stupid sod.

BOYLE. All right, all right! But can't ya help me?

MALLOY. For Christ's sake, give it here.

(She takes the bag from **RED HOOK**.*)*

Jesus, Red Hook, you smell like shite.

BOYLE. Well, it's a long way down, Maggie. And it's all wet and black as pitch down there. Why'd you have to tunnel so deep?

MALLOY. Because we had to get under the cellar that's under the Embassy you thickheaded brute. Under. The. Cellar. That's deep down. Now close up and cover it.

(He closes the trap with a resounding thud.)

Can you make any more noise you moron?

BOYLE. Sorry.

MALLOY. Cover it.

> (**BOYLE** *covers the trap with the carpet while* **MALLOY** *picks up the satchel.)*

> (**SHERLOCK HOLMES** *appears with a pistol in his hand.)*

HOLMES. I will take that satchel, madam.

> (**BOYLE** *starts to move.* **MAGGIE** *stares at* **HOLMES.***)*

Do not move, Mr. Boyle.

BOYLE. Not me, brother and sorry about last night – nothin' personal.

HOLMES. Yes, nothing personal about stabbing a man. Show me your hands, madam!

MALLOY. Plenty of men have pointed guns at me, mister, but I'm the one who is still standing above ground.

HOLMES. Yes, and if you wish to continue that relationship with the earth you will *show me your hands*!

> *(She shows him her hands. A little. She moves away from* **BOYLE***, widening the gap between them.)*

MALLOY. All right! All right, but there are two of us, you know and I'll be honest with you we both have pistols and even though this boy is a bit of a fool I know for a fact he's a dead shot so do you really think you can get both of us before you're dead?

HOLMES. Perhaps not but I promise you I will –

(The **PINKERTON** *comes silently into the room.)*

PINKS. It's two on two now, Maggie.

*(***PINKS** *disarms* **RED HOOK.***)*

MALLOY. Sonofabitch! All right, calm down gents, nobody wants to die. Mr. Boyle and I will just be on our way.

HOLMES. An excellent idea but leave the satchel, please.

MALLOY. No, sorry, we can't do that, mister. I don't get paid without I bring back this bag.

*(***ANNIE OAKLEY** *comes into the room, gun in hand.)*

ANNIE. You can't get paid if you're dead, Mrs. Malloy.

MALLOY. Goddammit! You again!

PINKS. Annie!

ANNIE. Don't start with me, Pinks. Hands up!

HOLMES. Wonderful. Their pistols, Mr. Pinks?

PINKS. I got it.

*(***PINKS** *disarms* **MAGGIE** *as* **HOLMES** *picks up the satchel; hefts it.)*

HOLMES. Of course. Perfect. Now, Mrs. Malloy, where is your master?

MALLOY. No man is my master.

HOLMES. No? *(Shouting.)* Hello! Hello! Hello! All ye, all ye walks in free! All ye, all ye walks in free!

*(***MYCROFT HOLMES** *comes in.)*

MYCROFT. Sherlock!

HOLMES. Brother!

MYCROFT. Damn you!

HOLMES. Mycroft, I am sorry –

MYCROFT. No sorrier than I.

HOLMES. – you must listen to me –

MYCROFT. Sherlock, give me that satchel and leave this place.

HOLMES. All right, yes, but we must leave together –

MYCROFT. No, Sherlock!

HOLMES. Mycroft, you don't understand –

MYCROFT. I understand perfectly. You promised not to be here and once again you have betrayed my trust.

HOLMES. Once again?

MYCROFT. I was foolish enough to imagine that you had decided to do the proper thing.

HOLMES. The proper thing being what you want?

MYCROFT. Yes!

HOLMES. When have I ever done that?

MYCROFT. Never!

HOLMES. Mycroft, please – come with me now!

MYCROFT. No, I must finish this.

HOLMES. Very well, then, we will talk here. Arnold Crofters!

MYCROFT. Sherlock, there is no time for this!

HOLMES. Tell me about Arnold Crofters.

MYCROFT. All right! For over two years Crofters had been one of my agents inside the Bank. At some point he took it into his head to betray me. It was he who facilitated the theft of the plates. I should have seen it. I did not.

HOLMES. The plates! Yes, these – *(He holds up the satchel.)* – are the printing plates for what – the ten pound note?

MYCROFT. Yes.

HOLMES. But why –?

MYCROFT. If millions of ten pound notes were flooded into the market in India or Afghanistan or Scotland for God's sake, the results for the Empire would have been catastrophic. I had to take the chance.

HOLMES. And you were given that chance because someone came to you with an offer.

MYCROFT. Sherlock –

HOLMES. Listen to me, Mycroft! Arnold Crofters. The Gas Explosion. Solomon Moses. The Mechanical Mole. Red Clay. The Briar Pipe. Ginger Biscuits and Don't Be Late.

MYCROFT. Brother –

HOLMES. When all those things slid together it was yellow.

MYCROFT. Yellow?

HOLMES. Yes.

MYCROFT. Then, please brother, for once in your life do as I ask: Give me the printing plates.

> *(**HOLMES** gives his brother the satchel. There is a little chuckle in the dark. It is **MAJOR RAMSEY**. **HOLMES** turns his pistol on him.)*

RAMSEY. I promise you, sir, I am unarmed. You assured me that you had your little brother in hand, Mr. Holmes.

MYCROFT. We had agreed that you would remain in the shadows, Major.

RAMSEY. Yes, but there was so much delightful activity out here in the light.

MYCROFT. I have the plates. You have your immunity. Our contract is fulfilled.

RAMSEY. You might remind your little brother of that fact.

MYCROFT. Sherlock, lower your pistol.

HOLMES. Mycroft, you can't seriously –

MYCROFT. Goddamnit, Sherlock, in the name of the Queen lower your pistol! All of you, lower your weapons.

> (**HOLMES, ANNIE,** *and the* **PINKS** *lower their guns.*)

Now, Major, you and your people may go.

RAMSEY. Thank you, Mr. Holmes. And may I say that it has been a privilege to work with you on this little project.

> (**RAMSEY** *pulls a steel pen-sized syringe from his pocket and smoothly places it against* **MYCROFT**'s *throat. Everyone tenses, guns are aimed.*)

Shoot and he dies! In this syringe is a pure tincture of a powerful South American herb. Once in your brother's system his heart will spasm in four seconds and he will be dead in five. Your weapons please.

> (**HOLMES** *puts down his pistol.* **ANNIE** *and the* **PINKS** *follow suit.* **MAGGIE** *grabs up a pistol and gives one to* **BOYLE.** *She then moves the group to one side.*)

MYCROFT. We had an agreement, Major.

RAMSEY. One which I now choose to ignore.

MYCROFT. If you kill us you will enjoy no immunity. They will run you to ground.

RAMSEY. Scotland Yard and the Home Office are of no concern to me. They are fools. This is very exciting, gentlemen, for tonight we will achieve a kind of numeric equilibrium. Chang, Crofters and Moses were the first to be subtracted. Then there was to be you, Mr. Mycroft Holmes, which brought the total to four – a rather dirty number. But with tonight's three additions the total comes to seven, which is not only a prime but it gleams like polished sterling.

> (**RAMSEY** *pulls the syringe away from* **MYCROFT**'s *throat and pushes him towards* **SHERLOCK**.)

MYCROFT. You were right, Sherlock. All yellow. Rory Siam.

HOLMES. Hans Jotnow, brother.

RAMSEY. Enough of your idioglossic nonsense. Mrs. Malloy. Mr. Boyle. Finish your job.

HOLMES. If you release us now, sir, I can vouch for your life. But if you press this matter I am genuinely afraid for your survival.

RAMSEY. I like that, sir, I do. Do you play chess?

HOLMES. Occasionally. I have had some difficulty in finding a worthy opponent.

MYCROFT. Hah!

RAMSEY. You have a champion's spirit, sir – finding yourself in a fatally weakened position you play the game as if you possessed the greatest advantage. I regret that we shall never play.

HOLMES. My position may not be as weak as you imagine.

RAMSEY. Look around you, sir. You have nothing. I own the day.

HOLMES. There is one thing that you shall never have, Major.

RAMSEY. What is that?

HOLMES. Watson!

> *(The trap door flies open and* **DR. JOHN HAMISH WATSON** *comes up with his revolver high and fires a shot.* **MALLOY** *and* **BOYLE** *begin to bring their guns to bear on* **WATSON.** *The* **PINKS** *bowls over* **BOYLE** *and gets his gun.* **ANNIE** *retrieves her weapon. There is a big struggle.)*

> *(***HOLMES** *grabs* **RAMSEY**'s *arm as he tries to stab* **MYCROFT** *with the poisonous syringe. While the other struggles resolve they fight for control of the syringe. Finally* **HOLMES** *has the upper hand and the point of the needle is at* **RAMSEY**'s *throat.)*

Checkmate, sir.

> *(Everyone is looking at the pair.* **HOLMES** *is poised to push the needle home.)*

MYCROFT. Sherlock...

HOLMES. Mycroft, you know what he is doing to London.

RAMSEY. Of course he knows. Your brother helped me do it!

MYCROFT. Sherlock, no –

HOLMES. He is responsible for the murder of at least three men.

MYCROFT. The security of the nation often demands sacrifice. That is the price I was forced to pay.

HOLMES. He planned to kill you, Mycroft.

MYCROFT. Yes, I know. But I am alive and we have the plates. I am sorry, Sherlock – truly I am – but the Queen has given her word.

HOLMES. This is not over between us.

RAMSEY. I sincerely hope not.

>(**HOLMES** *pulls the syringe away from* **RAMSEY***'s neck and releases him.*)

MYCROFT. You are free to go, Major.

>(**RAMSEY** *starts to leave.*)

ANNIE. *(To* **RAMSEY.***)* You killed Solomon Moses?

RAMSEY. Come, Mrs. Malloy. Mr. Boyle.

>(*She speaks louder.*)

ANNIE. You killed Solomon Moses?

RAMSEY. This really has become the most tiresome evening.

ANNIE. Mister! I need to know this for sure. Did you kill Solomon Moses?

RAMSEY. Young lady, in as much as I have the Queen's pardon for doing so I will happily state it more simply for you: yes, I killed Solomon Moses!

>(**ANNIE** *lifts her arm up. She holds a pistol in her hand. She fires two quick shots.* **RAMSEY** *shrieks and grabs first his left ear and then his right, which are bloodied.*)

Aaaaaahhhh!

PINKS. Jesus!

>(**MAGGIE** *and* **BOYLE** *scuttle out of the room.*)

WATSON. No!

PINKS. Annie!

ANNIE. You killed my brother.

MYCROFT. Miss Oakley, you musn't –

ANNIE. You killed my brother!

> *(She approaches* **RAMSEY** *who is standing, staring at her, mute.)*

PINKS. Annie!

ANNIE. Solomon was a criminal. He disgraced our family. He broke my mother's heart. But he didn't deserve to be butchered in an alley. He didn't deserve what you did to him!

> *(She cocks the pistol.* **RAMSEY** *just stares at her, blood dripping from his wounded ears as she draws a bead on him.)*

HOLMES. Miss Oakley. Annie. Annie! *(She looks at him.)* Please.

> *(***ANNIE** *holds her aim for a moment, then she very slowly lowers her pistol. She uncocks it, hands it to* **HOLMES** *–)*

ANNIE. Sorry Mr. Holmes.

> *(– and then hits* **RAMSEY** *square in the jaw.)*

He was my brother.

HOLMES. Yes.

MYCROFT. Major, I will see you to hospital.

RAMSEY. No! *(To* **MYCROFT.***)* As you stated earlier, sir, our contract is now complete.

> *(***RAMSEY,** *his ears bleeding and his lip cut, turns to* **HOLMES.***)*

But you and I, Mr. Sherlock Holmes, we shall continue our little game.

HOLMES. I look forward to it, sir.

RAMSEY. You kept your pawn hidden until the very last moment. Clever boy. I shan't forget that.

(He turns, smiling, bloody, and is gone.)

WATSON. Miss Oakley?

ANNIE. I've never actually fired a gun at a man before. I don't think I like it.

PINKS. C'mon. We should get back to the hotel.

ANNIE. Yes, I have to... Frank is home tomorrow. Dr. Watson.

WATSON. Goodnight, Miss Oakley.

ANNIE. Mr. Holmes – thank you.

HOLMES. Goodnight, Miss Oakley.

ANNIE. Gentlemen: Goodbye.

> *(**ANNIE** exits. **PINKS** gathers up any loose guns.)*

PINKS. We'll see ya.

> *(He exits.)*

MYCROFT. Good Lord. Americans and their guns.

HOLMES. Mycroft. What has become of Charlotte Lichter?

MYCROFT. She is safe and sound on board the steamship *Atlas*, with her Mechanical Mole, bound for New York. We should go, gentlemen. Gunshots from a bakeshop at two o'clock in the morning are sure to raise an alarm.

> *(**MYCROFT** picks up the satchel.)*

HOLMES. You knew Ramsey planned to kill you?

MYCROFT. I knew it was a probability. I was at fault, you see. I had to recover the plates.

HOLMES. Mycroft...

MYCROFT. Sherlock, you know as well as I that in our lives
we are rarely given the easy choice between good and
evil. In my line of work choosing the lesser of two evils
can be a rare pleasure. More often than not, however,
I am forced to choose the evil we can survive. Good
night, brother.

> (**MYCROFT** *exits.* **HOLMES** *collapses into a*
> *chair.* **WATSON** *stands looking at him. Music*.*
> *The scene changes around them. Barnes and*
> *Finlay disappears and Baker Street coalesces.*
> *Lights up on:)*

---

* A license to produce *Sherlock Holmes and The American Problem* does
not include a performance license for any third-party or copyrighted
music. Licensees should create an original composition or use music in
the public domain. For further information, please see the Music and
Third Party Materials Use Note on page iii.

Scene Five

(Baker Street, the next morning. **HOLMES** *is sitting in the chair he collapsed into the previous night.* **WATSON** *stands looking at him.* **MRS. HUDSON** *enters. She puts her hand on the coffee pot.)*

MRS. HUDSON. Some fresh coffee, Mr. Holmes?

(No response.)

Perhaps you would care for a little breakfast now?

(No response. **MRS. HUDSON** *shrugs at* **WATSON.** *This is certainly not the first time that* **SHERLOCK HOLMES** *has behaved oddly but still, it concerns her.)*

Will you be swimming the channel this morning, Mr. Holmes, or are you taking the boat-train to France?

(Beat.)

HOLMES. Don't be stupid, woman. The tides are westerly off Dover this morning and so unsuitable to a manual crossing.

MRS. HUDSON. Oh. Well. I see.

*(***MRS. HUDSON** *exits.* **WATSON** *loses his patience with* **HOLMES.***)*

WATSON. All right, Holmes. That's enough.

HOLMES. What?

WATSON. You've sat there all night like a stone lion, not saying two words to anyone. Mrs. Hudson was good enough to make you a late supper last night of your favorite Kedgeree, which you didn't thank her for which was no great surprise but then didn't touch and so she thought you were dying. This morning she has made you coffee and toast, which, again, you have not touched. I suppose you have a perfect right to be glum and silent but you have just intentionally been rude to her and so now, Holmes, you really must rouse yourself from this particular brown study into which you have fallen and tell me – what in God's name is the matter now?

HOLMES. I failed, Watson.

WATSON. Failed? Holmes, despite the best efforts of two brilliant minds – this Professor fellow and your brother – you managed to uncover the solution to the most complex problem imaginable.

HOLMES. Yes, yes, I know. I was slow to the game, but I got there at last. No, that's not it.

WATSON. What then?

HOLMES. I failed my brother.

WATSON. But Holmes – how?

HOLMES. When Mycroft came to us with that improbable invitation it was patently obvious to me that the exhibition at Seamore Place was a ruse. An intentionally clumsy ruse. And I knew that Mycroft knew that I knew. I understood perfectly what he was asking of me.

WATSON. What?

HOLMES. He was asking me to...no – no, by visiting me in my rooms and thereby turning decades of precedence on its head – he was *begging* me, begging me not to be where I was bound to be. Begging me instead to go to the exhibition. To sip champagne. To gaze at Uncle Emile's horrid paintings. To be miserable. To be *safe*. But I didn't want to be warned off by my older brother. No, I had the bit firmly between my teeth and I was going to see this matter to its end regardless of what he wanted. And in doing so I very nearly got all of us killed.

WATSON. Holmes, don't be a fool.

HOLMES. What?

WATSON. *You saved your brother's life.*

> (**WATSON** *turns and walks to the table.*)

HOLMES. Oh.

> (*Beat.*)

Tell me, Watson.

WATSON. Yes?

HOLMES. How long had you been waiting?

WATSON. Where?

HOLMES. Under that trapdoor.

WATSON. Waiting? What do you mean, waiting? I was just coming up that blasted ladder in the pitch dark when I heard you shout my name!

HOLMES. Perfect timing, then.

WATSON. Holmes, you know for a fact that was too fine a thing by half!

HOLMES. Yes, but you did it –

WATSON. And if you ever do something like that again –

HOLMES. Watson –

WATSON. – I swear to God I will shoot you myself!

HOLMES. Fair enough. But it was something of a thrill, wasn't it?

> (**MRS. HUDSON** *enters with a small wrapped parcel.*)

MRS. HUDSON. Gentlemen, will you be in for dinner this evening?

WATSON. Oh, well, I –

HOLMES. Mrs. Hudson?

(*He gets an addressed envelope from the mantel or somewhere.*)

MRS. HUDSON. Yes, Mr. Holmes?

HOLMES. Might you give this to the boy to be posted?

HUDSON. Very well. (*Looks at the envelope.*) Oh, to Miss Oakley?

HOLMES. Yes. And Mrs. Hudson – is it too late for breakfast?

HUDSON. Of course not, Mr. Holmes. I'll have it right up.

HOLMES. Thank you, Mrs. Hudson.

(MRS. HUDSON *takes that precious "Thank you" and exits.*)

WATSON. What are you sending to Miss Oakley?

HOLMES. Her cheque for a hundred pounds.

WATSON. She won't be happy about that.

HOLMES. That is entirely up to her.

WATSON. Miss Annie Oakley. She really is something extraordinary, isn't she?

HOLMES. Yes. Beautiful, charming, deadly with a pistol and a chronic liar. The best sort of American, I think.

WATSON. Oh, now, Holmes, really –

HOLMES. I am joking, Watson. You are quite right – she is a truly remarkable woman.

(MRS. HUDSON *comes breezing into the room carrying a huge tray filled with their breakfast.*)

HUDSON. Your breakfast, gentlemen. Although I'm not sure real gentlemen take their breakfast this late in the morning.

HOLMES. Thank you for humouring us, Mrs. Hudson.

MRS. HUDSON. Of course, Mr. Holmes.

WATSON. Yes, thank you Mrs. Hudson.

> *(She deposits plates and platters and a covered hot dish.)*

HOLMES. Might we have a fresh pot of coffee?

MRS. HUDSON. Of course you may.

> *(She exits to get more coffee.)*

HOLMES. Well. Now, would you care for some eggs, Watson?

> *(They pass food around.)*

WATSON. Oh, Mrs. Hudson's coddled eggs. Capital. Thank you, Holmes.

> *(**HOLMES** pauses mid-pass.)*

HOLMES. And thank you, Watson.

WATSON. Hmm? For what?

HOLMES. Well...for...you know...for...saving my life.

WATSON. Oh, well. Yes...yes...of course. Right. Potatoes?

HOLMES. Yes, for God's sake, please.

WATSON. All right, Holmes, you may as well tell me.

HOLMES. Tell you what?

WATSON. What in God's name happened?

HOLMES. Oh. Well. I will have a tomato, thank you. Now, let's see: Major Ramsey stole the printing plates by using Arnold Crofters to gain access to the Bank of England, and then Solomon Moses to breach the vault and make off with one set of the plates which Ramsey then sold to the American Ambassador who desperately wanted to take his revenge on the British Crown because of his missing arm.

WATSON. What? What about his missing arm? Toast?

HOLMES. Please. Well, I learned just yesterday that he lost that arm rather late in their Civil War and he became convinced that if only Her Majesty's government had more forcefully supported the Union the war would have ended earlier.

WATSON. Ah, and he would still have his arm.

HOLMES. Just so.

WATSON. Butter?

HOLMES. Thank you. The man is obsessed. By his lights it was not General Lee but the Queen herself who took his arm.

WATSON. I see. Marmalade?

HOLMES. Not just yet. Now, at about the same time the plates were sold Charlotte Lichter's Mechanical Mole was stolen, reassembled at Francis Street and began tunneling towards the American Embassy.

WATSON. So Ramsey used the Mechanical Mole to steal the printing plates for the ten pound note from the American Embassy that he had stolen two weeks earlier from the Bank of England?

HOLMES. Precisely. And here, Watson, we come to the raison d'etre of this singularly brilliant plan: Major Ramsey approached the Home Office with an offer: He was in a position to recover the printing plates but there would, of course, be a *price*. He must be granted absolute immunity for any actions taken during the recovery period. The Crown accepted his offer. He then decapitated the criminal heads of the metropolis and his ascendancy as overlord of the London underworld was essentially assured. Now the marmalade, please.

WATSON. Dear God. What a mind.

HOLMES. Yes. These eggs are first rate.

WATSON. Lovely. And what do we have here?

> *(He opens a basket covered by a checkered linen towel.)*

Ah, splendid. Scones!

HOLMES. Your favorite, eh?

WATSON. My great weakness, I'm afraid.

> *(He breaks one in half, smells it.)*

Oh! Almond, I think? And some lemon, perhaps? That's something new.

> *(He starts buttering the scone as* **MRS. HUDSON** *returns with the coffee.)*

HUDSON. Here is your coffee, gentlemen.

HOLMES. Oh, capital.

WATSON. And almond scones, Mrs. Hudson? That's new for you, isn't it?

MRS. HUDSON. Oh, they're not mine, gentlemen.

WATSON. No?

MRS. HUDSON. No. They're from *Barnes and Finlay*. I thought one of you must have ordered them.

> *(***WATSON** *is about to bite the scone.* **HOLMES** *grabs his arm mid-bite.)*

HOLMES. Watson, no!

WATSON. Holmes –

HOLMES. Did you order the scones, Watson?

WATSON. No.

HOLMES. Nor did I.

> *(He takes the scone from* **WATSON** *and smells it.)*

Yes. Not almonds. Potassium of Cyanide.

MRS. HUDSON. Oh dear.

HOLMES. Wipe your hands, Watson.

WATSON. Right. Good God.

HOLMES. Mrs. Hudson, you've not tasted these, have you?

MRS. HUDSON. No.

> *(***HOLMES** *puts the scone back in the basket with the others and hands them to* **MRS. HUDSON.** *He still holds the checkered linen towel.)*

HOLMES. Put these back in the box with the others – don't touch them – and wash your hands immediately.

MRS. HUDSON. Yes. I am so sorry, gentlemen.

HOLMES. Nothing to be sorry about, Mrs. Hudson. We're all well.

MRS. HUDSON. Thank God for that. I'll bring up some toast, shall I? I baked the bread myself!

> *(She exits holding the basket like an armed bomb.)*

WATSON. Good God, Holmes. Was it that Ramsey fellow?

HOLMES. Of course. He did promise that our game would continue. Although I am somewhat surprised that his next move came so quickly.

WATSON. What are we going to do now, Holmes?

HOLMES. Well, first, Watson, we are going to finish our excellent breakfast.

WATSON. Right. Right. Near fatal poisoning always sharpens my appetite.

HOLMES. Yes. Here, have a rasher of bacon.

WATSON. Thank you.

> (**HOLMES** *sees the checkered cloth that came in with the scones. He picks it up and then gazes up at the ceiling for a moment. Some parts of a puzzle are coming together.*)

HOLMES. Watson.

WATSON. Yes?

HOLMES. Prepare yourself.

WATSON. What? Oh. Oh, yes. You mean your, your anagramantics.

HOLMES. Yes. Yes. Major T.I. Ramsey.

WATSON. Oh. Major T.I. Ramsey.

> (*They look at each other for a long moment. Then:*)

Marjorie Tamsy.

HOLMES. Very good, Watson.

WATSON. Thank you, Holmes. And –?

HOLMES. It is a kind of checkered thing. Hard and tastes of licorice – James Moriarty.

WATSON. Oh.

HOLMES. Yes. Professor James Moriarty.

WATSON. Do you think that really is his name?

HOLMES. We shall see, Watson. We shall see.

>   *(A breath.)*

Coffee?

>   *(Music*. Lights fade.)*

End of Play

---

* A license to produce *Sherlock Holmes and The American Problem* does not include a performance license for any third-party or copyrighted music. Licensees should create an original composition or use music in the public domain. For further information, please see the Music and Third Party Materials Use Note on page iii.